her spy to have

book one, spy games series

PAULA
ALTENBURG

This book is a work of fiction. The characters, incidents, and dialogue are drawn from the author's imagination and are not real. Any resemble to actual events or persons, living or dead, is entirely coincidental.

Published by Paula Altenburg
Stewiacke, Nova Scotia Canada
B0N 2J0

Copyright © 2016 by Paula Altenburg
Cover design by Syd Gill/Syd Gill Designs
Interior formatting by Author E.M.S.
Edited by Nancy Cassidy/The Red Pen Coach

ISBN: 978-0-9937166-0-7
www.paulaaltenburg.com

Printed in the U.S.A.

"International intrigue, adversaries with more in common than they want to admit, and ohhhh the chemistry...I couldn't put *Her Spy To Have* down!"

"Why do you do this?" she asked.

"Do what?"

"Follow me around. Look at me as if you find me fascinating. Touch me, and say nice things to me. And then, you pull away as if you did nothing at all." She gave him a self-deprecating smile. "I've already agreed to tell you everything I know. There's no need for these games."

He didn't deny it, as she'd expected him to. He didn't look sorry for it, either. He raked fingers through his sun-streaked hair, spiking it in the front. He looked like an older version of Kiefer, but much sexier.

And far more dangerous to her peace of mind.

"I do it because I can't help it," he confessed. His eyes glittered. "You seem to bring out the worst in me."

She could say the same about what he did to her. She'd never had a problem with insecurity, or of second-guessing herself, before he came along. All she could do was continue to pretend that he didn't affect her. That her heart didn't race when he looked at her that way.

"Do your worst, then," she said. "One of these days I'm going to call you on it."

His voice dropped, developing a seductive edge to it that sent a frisson of awareness through her body. "You don't want to do that."

She clenched her fingers more tightly together. "No?"

"Absolutely not." He reached for the door, popping it open. "You might discover I'm not bluffing."

"Wait a moment."

He paused, half turning, one foot already on the ground. Amusement—and something more—lit his eyes as they met hers. "You're calling me on it already?"

CHAPTER ONE

Bangkok, Thailand

"CHAN ME PASSPORT CANADA, tha ja kai, khun ja seu tao rai ka?"

How much for the Canadian passport?

Isabelle spoke fast, her Thai barely adequate, her understanding of it less so, and tried to sound confident. The hustle and noise of the vendors and patrons of Khao San Road, the center of tourism in Bangkok, did nothing to help her concentration. The heat and humidity were two levels beyond tolerable. The heavy scent of spices from the street cart shielding the transaction from onlookers made her mouth water and her stomach rumble. She hadn't eaten all day.

The market was crowded this evening. She'd counted on it. Nightclubs had opened their doors, the neon signs bright against a backdrop of tall buildings and patchy sky. Ragged hawkers stood on the street and handed out flyers announcing the various entertainment options available inside. As soon as she got her money, she could disappear in the confusion.

The young man in worn jeans and gray, sleeveless T-shirt appeared to grasp her meaning well enough. Straight black hair tickled his brow as he glanced around, then made an unmistakable gesture with his fingers. *Show me.*

Isabelle's father hadn't raised an idiot. That passport wasn't coming out of hiding until she had the money for it within grabbing distance. Her hostel was only five dollars US a night, but other than a few *bhat*, that was now three dollars more than she owned. She had a few other things she could hawk which would pay for another night or two, but they wouldn't bring in enough money to get her back to Canada. The document was all she had of any value. From here she planned to go to the Canadian Embassy and report it stolen.

She pretended not to understand him. Instead, she tapped two fingers on the back pocket of her shorts to indicate yes, she had the passport on her, and to give him the impression that was where it was stored, when in fact, it was safely taped to her stomach.

"You speak English?" the man asked.

"*Un petit peu,*" she replied. "*Mais je suis française.*" *A little. But I am French.* She didn't want to be able to communicate with him too well just yet. "How much?" she repeated, again in Thai.

He named a ridiculous, lowball amount. It was worth far more than that, as Isabelle was well aware. She made a counteroffer—hers, much too high.

His dark eyes flitted past her left shoulder, just for a split second, but it was warning enough. She knew what was coming and been expecting it.

Someone jostled her from behind, knocking her off balance. A light hand slid across her buttocks. Isabelle felt the faux leather passport holder—with its wad of folded tourist flyers inside—being lifted from the pocket she'd tapped.

The pickpocket was okay, but she'd known better ones. She'd once met a Roma in Italy who could pull the money from an open wallet, right under the owner's nose. She didn't turn around, or indicate in any way that she knew she'd been robbed, but kept her attention on her target.

"I've changed my mind. I'm not interested in buying," the man said to her.

Isabelle switched to English. "It will be your loss, then. I can't imagine your friend will make much profit off a few tourist maps of the Grand Palace."

Surprise flashed in his eyes, followed by a grudging admiration that lifted the corners of his lips, creasing smooth, buttered-toffee skin. "I see we speak a common language after all. Who told you to come to me?"

"I'd rather not say."

In fact, no one had told her. For three days, Isabelle had wandered through the businesses and street stalls of Khao San Road, quietly ferreting out the information she needed. She'd studied the people who worked here, seen who met with whom, and what exchanged hands.

It had been far too easy. She'd spent her entire life learning how to blend into crowds. With nondescript brown eyes and unremarkable, olive-toned skin, hers was the kind of face that didn't attract a lot of attention in a city like this. She was of medium height, slight but not skinny, and she wore her straight, dark hair scraped back in a high ponytail. She could pass as Italian, Spanish, or French—and spoke each language fluently, as well as English. Her passport claimed she was French Canadian, and it was the language she spoke with her father, but Isabelle hadn't spent many of her twenty-four years in her home province of Quebec. She and her father had moved around a lot, on three different continents.

And now he was missing.

He hadn't shown up in Thailand to meet her as planned, and he'd left no messages for her. Isabelle was worried sick. Their fallback plan in such an event was always for her to head to Canada and wait for him to track her down. Isabelle, however, had been fired by the British couple who'd hired her as an au pair, then abandoned in Bangkok to fend for herself. They'd refused to pay her final month's wages, too.

Bastards.

She'd waited for her father longer than she should have, and now, unless this plan worked, she wasn't going anywhere.

The young Thai studied her for a few seconds. She stared back. She wasn't afraid for her safety. The only thing separating them from the horde of tourists wandering Khao San was a flimsy cart selling shrimp and crispy rice salad, and a few racks of T-shirts covered by three large umbrellas. She wasn't above making a scene if she felt at all threatened. She did worry about losing her passport and not getting her money, though.

Five minutes later, they agreed on a price.

She lifted the hem of her drab, khaki-colored T-shirt and peeled the passport off her belly, then held it tight in one hand, close to her chest. She listened for hurried footsteps behind her, or anything out of the ordinary, but the street was noisy with music and people.

She made him count the money for her. He held it out. As she reached for it with one hand, she extended the passport in the other.

His eyes flickered up. They widened.

Isabelle tried to snatch the passport back, but someone caught hold of her wrist.

Garrett Downing had seen people do a lot of stupid things over the course of his career, but this was one of the best.

The boy with the money ducked behind the shrimp cart, thrusting aside heavily laden racks of bright T-shirts. Seconds later, he was gone. The vendor of the cart shouted after him, her irritation plain, although Garrett had no doubt the two were well known to each other. She had to be aware of what types of transactions were occurring behind her. The boy hadn't selected this spot to do business at random.

The girl yanked her arm, trying to break free of his grip. When it was obvious he wasn't about to let go, she sucked in a deep breath.

"Go ahead and scream for help," Garrett said, cutting her off. He'd stepped in close so that to anyone passing by, it looked like they were deep in a domestic dispute. "I'd be interested to hear you explain this to the local police."

She muttered something rude in Italian but he wasn't so easily fooled. "That's a Canadian passport you were about to sell. You either own it or you stole it. I doubt if you'd be as eager to draw attention to us by screaming if you stole it, so I'm pretty sure it's yours and you speak English." His fingers tightened on the fine bones of her slender wrist, not in an attempt to hurt her, but to show her he was serious about not letting go. "What the hell were you thinking?"

She stood her ground. "What I think—or do—is no business of yours."

There could be a Thai boyfriend behind her imprudent decision—someone who'd convinced her she wanted to stay in the country to be with him, then set up this exchange for her. She wouldn't be the first girl to fall for that ploy.

She'd handled the transaction like a pro, however. The majority of girls would be in tears at this point. He had no idea what her real game was and the mystery intrigued him.

"Maybe not for most things," he agreed, "but what you do with that passport is. I'm with the Canadian Embassy."

Her long-lashed eyes, a deep brown, raked him from head to toe. She started to laugh. He could understand why she found that so improbably funny. He was dressed in a green printed, button-down shirt, Tilley cargo shorts, and a pair of Ecco sandals, looking every inch the North American tourist, not diplomat, but what he'd told her wasn't a lie. It simply wasn't the whole truth. He really was with the Canadian Embassy, working out of the Defence attaché's office while on assignment, but as an intelligence officer for CSIS, the Canadian Security Intelligence Service. He'd been in Thailand for more than a month now, investigating the theft of Canadian Department of National Defence property. Rumor had it that parts for weapons systems—meaning aircraft with nuclear capabilities—were being smuggled through maintenance contractors in Thailand, then shipped out on a convoluted route to Pakistan. He needed to figure out the path and the players. He'd come to Khao San tonight to meet an informant who hadn't shown.

So Garrett was already annoyed when he'd stumbled on her foolish transaction. He reached into one of the zippered pockets on his shorts and pulled out his billfold. He flipped it open to his ID and showed it to her.

That wiped the smile from her face.

He shoved it back in his pocket. He plucked the passport from her fingers and looked at the picture and name. The passport then followed the billfold into his shorts pocket. "Well, Isabelle Beausejour. Let's hear your explanation. I'll bet it's good."

She deflated before his eyes, all the brash bravery gone. On the surface, she was ordinary enough. Smooth, light-olive skin. Even, unremarkable features. Dark, straight, unspectacular hair scraped into a cheerleader-style ponytail. Cheap shorts and T-shirt, the same standard uniform as all the international backpackers roaming Bangkok wore. Nothing about her explained this sudden alertness she caused in him—the spiking of interest that made him feel...*greasy*, was the best way to describe it. Like he was ogling a teenage girl in a schoolyard. He resisted the urge to check her passport again for her age. Eighteen, perhaps?

His thirty-one seemed so old by comparison.

"I was hungry," she whispered.

While that was no doubt the truth, it was hardly the whole of it. He refused to feel pity as he debated what he should do about this situation. No harm had been done. If he let her go, she'd try to sell the passport again, he didn't doubt it, but after his intervention just now, she'd find it much more difficult.

But she was hungry.

Not my problem.

His meeting was more important. He needed the intelligence he'd come to collect. He checked his watch. Which wasn't going to happen tonight. The informant wouldn't show now. Moreover, if he'd seen even a part of what had just happened, he'd stay far away.

Inside, Garrett sighed. Spare him from stupid people who made unfathomable life choices. He'd spent weeks chasing this lead. All of that careful work, gone. Then, a grudging pity took hold of his heart. He'd never been hungry a day in his life.

"Let's get you something to eat." He bit back his frustration. It wasn't as if he had anything better to do at the moment.

He slid his palm down her wrist to her hand until their fingers laced together, as if they were lovers out for a stroll. She stiffened, but didn't pull away. He'd have paid money to know what was going through her head at that moment.

They got caught up in a swarm of German tourists who were loud, drunk, and enjoying themselves to the entertainment of everyone they met on the street. Garrett pulled the girl to his side, shielding her with his larger frame, but also to keep them from becoming separated. Bodies bumped against him. Someone mumbled sorry. And then they were free.

They walked to a small Thai café he knew on Phra Athit Road, where the street was less crowded so they could talk, and sat at a table outdoors. Garrett ordered pork soup and noodles for them both, as well as some stuffed flat breads and a couple of iced colas. His shirt stuck to his back. He loved the food in this city, but the humidity and heat had been the hardest things about Bangkok for him to adapt to. While Ottawa, Ontario sweltered in the summertime, it was nothing like this.

He scooped up a spoonful of soup. "I'm waiting for an explanation."

She sat very straight, her spine not touching the back of her chair, looking more poised than tense. Despite the hunger he could read in her eyes, and the faint hollows in her cheeks, she picked at her bread, barely eating. "I came to Bangkok four months ago to work as a nanny for a British couple. Two weeks ago, the wife caught her husband trying to kiss me in a corner of the garden. I was dismissed on the spot without final wages."

The lack of embellishment, and the faint bitterness beneath her words, told him everything. The story wasn't uncommon. The only thing he questioned was how willing a participant she'd been in the garden fiasco, and that was none of his business. "Why not go to the Embassy for help?"

She sipped a little soup from her spoon before answering. "I planned to, but I needed to have money to get back to Canada. I was going to sell the passport, then go to them and report it stolen. They'd have issued me a temporary one."

Her plan was bad on so many levels. Not to mention, a federal offense that could well lead to jail time. He had to ask himself what sort of person thought to sell a passport. She'd almost pulled it off, too.

There was also that two-week period of time since her dismissal. It made no sense.

"You have no family to call? Friends?" he persisted.

Again, she hesitated. "There's just my father, and he travels a lot. I'm not sure how to reach him."

Beausejour...

Garrett had a good memory and there was something about the name that rang a bell. He'd seen it somewhere else recently. A CSIS case file, perhaps.

Then he had it. Marc Beausejour was a suspected middleman in the theft of Canadian government property. There had been little information on him in the file, if he recalled correctly, mostly because Beausejour was a simple link in a very long, complex chain.

Garrett tapped the table with an index finger, his thoughts racing. Perhaps not so simple as was first believed. What a coincidence that a girl bearing his name, with the same transient lifestyle, happened to be in Bangkok at a time coinciding with a CSIS investigation of the smuggling of Canadian military goods across international borders.

"What's your father's name?" he asked.

"Leon." She gave it a French pronunciation, *Lee-onh*, with the accent on the heavily nasal second syllable.

The name was wrong, but that didn't mean a whole lot. He wished he could remember if Marc Beausejour had a middle name, or another he went by. "What does he do?"

She shrugged slender shoulders beneath the shapeless, oversize T-shirt she wore. "Something in international business. For a security management company, I believe."

"What's the name of the company?"

"I have no idea."

He set down his spoon, finally giving in to impatience. "Look, Isabelle. I could have turned you over to the authorities. Instead, I'm trying to help you. A little cooperation on your part would be nice."

She raised dark, unreadable eyes from the contents of her bowl, which she'd been examining with an intense and frowning concentration. "I'm an adult. My father and I are no longer as close as we once were. When he wants to see me, he finds me. I'm sorry if my lack of reliable friends is an inconvenience for you. I have plenty, I assure you, but none I feel comfortable enough with to call and ask for several thousand dollars that I probably won't be able to pay back."

His impatience dissolved. She was scared. More than that, she was defensive, and trying to deflect his attention away from her father. She was protecting him.

Too many coincidences.

He had her passport, which should have emergency contact information, but he didn't want to spook her any more than she already was by checking it in front of her. Besides, it was undoubtedly false. If her father was connected to his investigation, and his instincts said he was, then keeping track of her might be the best way to find him.

And it would be easiest to do that if she were in Canada.

He still had her passport. She had to get it back.

Her fingers burned from where he'd been holding her hand. The name on the ID he'd shown her read Garrett Downing. Despite the ugly and tasteless shirt, he was a nice-looking man. Broad-shouldered, not quite six feet tall, and physically fit, he was built more like a wrestler than a runner. He had short brown hair, bleached at the tips by the sun. A bump and slight bend to an otherwise straight nose indicated it must have been broken at least once, giving him a "Don't mess with me," air. He probably wasn't as old as he'd have people believe. Isabelle was good at guessing ages and she placed his at around thirty.

And he was smart.

She had lived abroad for years. Ex-pats heard things. Mr. Downing, she suspected, was with CSIS, which meant he was a spy. That was the only reason she could think of for why he'd be working at the Canadian Embassy, yet hanging out in Khao San at this time of night wearing those ridiculous clothes. Plus, Khao San wasn't a place where foreigners spent more than a day or so, really, and he obviously knew the area reasonably well. She didn't get the vibe of a man interested in late night sex shows, or child prostitutes, either. He paid close attention to his surroundings, radiating an intensity that kept her on edge, as if she were waiting for a bomb to go off or some other tragedy to strike. His eyes, a clear, hazel color in the artificial lighting, never stopped moving. She'd bet he could tell her the exact number of tuk-tuks— unauthorized taxis that looked like three-wheeled golf carts—that had gone past since they sat down. That was how he'd noticed what she'd been doing.

CSIS. Without a doubt.

He was asking too many questions. Those hazel eyes had fixed on her face in a way she didn't like when they spoke of her father. She searched through everything she'd said and could find nothing that would warrant such a reaction. She loved her father deeply. It had been just the two of them for as long as she could remember. But from the age of fourteen, she'd known his work for an international security management company occasionally skated on the fringes of the law, offering protection to people who might not deserve it. Thank God she knew nothing about his recent activities—or current whereabouts.

She forced herself to eat even though her appetite was long gone. She had no idea when she might get another meal, and it gave her time to think. Even if Mr. Righteous saw her deported back to Canada, she'd have nothing when she got there. No money. No home. No family except for grandparents she hadn't seen since she was a very small child, and who'd expressed no interest in her. Educated in a number of boarding schools, and sometimes by satellite from remote locations, her friendships, casual at best, spanned three continents. But Canada was where her father wanted her to go if they were ever separated, so that's what she intended to do. Besides, it was far better to be destitute in Canada than penniless on the streets of Bangkok. The thought of ending up in one of the local strip shows in order to feed herself didn't appeal in the least.

"Where do you think your father is now?"

Isabelle lifted a napkin to her lips, then crumpled it in her hand. "I don't see what relevance this has, Mr. Downing. I'm an adult," she repeated. "He's not my keeper."

"Garrett."

That threw her off, and she slipped into her native French without thinking. "*Pardon?*"

"Call me Garrett. And it is relevant. How old are you, Isabelle?" He cast a disarming, crooked grin her way that unsettled her further. "Don't make me check your passport."

"I'm twenty-four."

She could tell that surprised him, which came as no shock. She knew very well how young she looked. How plain. Women who traveled alone as much as she did went out of their way not to draw too much attention to themselves. She'd broken that rule today.

She ran through what she knew—or at least suspected—in her head. He was no doubt CSIS. He was curious about her father, who'd planned to meet her in Bangkok. And her father was missing.

But what if she was wrong and Garrett Downing wasn't CSIS, or even with the Embassy at all? What if he was something else entirely? And what if he hadn't stumbled on her by accident, but because he'd been looking for her?

How much trouble was her father in?

She itched to examine his ID more closely.

"I'd like my passport back," she said.

"I can sympathize with your situation. I really can. Well," he amended. "Trying to sell your passport, not so much." His eyes glittered with humor, making him seem more human and less like a spy. Or killer. Worse, a white slaver. "But unfortunately, the best I can do for you is to help collect your belongings and escort you to the airport. You can have it back once we get there."

"I have no money," Isabelle reminded him.

"I'm going to buy your ticket for you." He held up a hand before she could interrupt. "I'm also going to go to the gate with you, make sure you get on the plane, and have someone waiting for you when you arrive in Canada. I can at least help get you back on your feet."

Tears of relief, hot and unexpected, welled in her eyes. Then a lifetime of caution reasserted itself. The possibility of white slavery wasn't a joke. She blinked the tears away. "Why would you want to help me?"

This time, he was the one to hesitate. "I have two sisters. I'd hate to see one of them in your situation."

She wasn't a lost twelve-year-old. He had another motive, one he didn't plan to share with her. She could hardly question him about it.

Or turn down his offer, either.

The sweating glasses of cola had left large rings of water on the table. Isabelle dabbed at them with the crumpled napkin still clutched in her fingers. "I can't pay you back."

"I don't expect you to." He finished the last piece of flatbread and washed it down with his drink. He flashed that grin at her again. "Besides, there's a good chance that whoever meets you at the airport will confiscate your passport again."

CHAPTER TWO

Nova Scotia, Canada, one month later

KIEFER MANSFORD, THREE YEARS old and squealing with glee, did a running cannonball off the diving board that never failed to make Isabelle's heart stutter no matter how many times his mother assured her he could swim like a fish. He landed with a splash, washing a tidal wave of water onto his shrieking older sisters, Beth and Chelsea, who were dipping their toes at the side of the pool.

The toddler popped to the surface, a huge grin on his face.

Beth, seven, plopped her hands on her hips and did an excellent impression of her mother. "If you do that again, you'll be sorry." Kiefer stuck out his tongue. "Izzy, make him stop!" she demanded.

"The best way to make him stop," Isabelle said, "is to get in the pool."

Five-year-old Chelsea, her saucy red curls already spilling out of the ponytail Isabelle had fashioned only moments before, folded her arms across her chest and stuck out her lip. "The water's too cold."

"The pool is heated."

It was also early July in Nova Scotia. The afternoon temperature had already topped ninety degrees and was steadily climbing, and for her part, Isabelle was more than happy to get wet and cool off. The children's mother wanted them tired out and ready for an early bedtime because they had a surprise guest arriving. If a swim didn't wear them out, the gorgeous, family-friendly backyard provided plenty of other entertainment options for three active children.

She'd been with the Mansfords less than a month, but she'd already learned the best way to get the girls to cooperate was to start having fun.

"Kiefer's got the right idea. I'm going in." She headed for the diving board. She was adjusting her bikini top, making sure it was secure, when she heard male voices in the house, near the open patio doors off the deck.

"Daddy's home!" blonde-headed Beth shrieked. She and Chelsea ran for the house, ponytails swinging and bobbing in tandem.

Isabelle stepped off the board and scooted around the side of the pool to help Kiefer out of the water, grabbing a towel off one of the lounge chairs as she passed, conscious she was wearing nothing but a few scraps of colorful fabric linked together by string. She hadn't bothered bringing a wrap outdoors with her because the house was supposed to be empty all day. While far from conservative, when it came to her body she'd learned to be cautious around her employers.

She was lifting Kiefer's slippery, round little frame from the pool and drying him off with the towel so he wouldn't track water through the house when the patio screen slid back and footsteps could be heard on the deck behind her.

The girls' cries of "Daddy!" quickly shifted to squeals

of "Uncle Garrett!" and an even higher level of agitated excitement, if that were possible. Kiefer struggled free and darted for the deck, leaving Isabelle with the damp towel clutched in her hands.

Garrett. A sense of impending doom crawled around the pit of her stomach.

I have two sisters.

Never, in a million years, and given the circumstances under which they'd met, would she have considered the possibility he'd arrange for her to work for one of them. *Please let it not be him.*

She turned around.

And there he was.

She hadn't seen him since Bangkok. This time, instead of CSIS, everything about Garrett Downing screamed money. He still wore the Tilley shorts, but the Ecco sandals and ugly tourist shirt were gone. He'd replaced them with soft leather, slip-on driving shoes and a dove-gray polo shirt. On his left wrist he wore a diver's wristwatch that no doubt cost more than she'd earned in the entire past year. Familiar hazel eyes, as direct and all-seeing as she remembered, met hers over the children's heads, just for a second, but long enough to ratchet up her anxiety level. He didn't seem at all pleased to see her, which struck her as odd, since her being here hadn't been her idea. But it was his look of surprise as it traveled from her face to linger at the glittering navel piercing above her bikini bottom that annoyed her, although she couldn't say why.

He'd escorted her to the airport and seen her off, just as he'd said he would. She'd been met at the Ottawa airport by an off-duty RCMP officer who'd shown her his ID and politely asked for her passport, then chauffeured her to a downtown hotel and said she could order room service if she was hungry. The next day Peter Mansford, a Nova Scotia Member of Parliament, had arrived to see her, and after a two-hour interview, offered her a position as nanny to his three children for the summer.

She'd liked Peter at once. He had a quiet manner, very polite, and when she'd met his wife Cheryl, she'd liked her, too. Still, it wasn't as if she'd had a whole lot of choice in accepting the offer. While his name had never been mentioned, it was clear Garrett intended to keep close tabs on her. Right now, pleasant as it was, Isabelle was under what was unquestionably an unofficial house arrest.

She wrapped the towel around her hips so she wouldn't feel quite so naked. Either she was under arrest or she wasn't. There was only one way to find out. She crossed the wet grass between the pool and the deck, and while the children mobbed their father, thrust out her hand to his guest.

"Mr. Downing," she said. "We meet again."

It turned out that Isabelle Beausejour had hidden layers. He didn't recall her being quite so...attractive.

The entire package appealed to him, he decided, once the initial shock wore off. On the surface, there was nothing remarkable about her, but there was nothing displeasing, either. Average height, average features, average coloring. Brown hair, brown eyes. If she were a bird, she'd be a pretty little wood thrush. The toned body was what caught him off guard. So did the navel jewelry.

He'd asked Peter to check her references and find her work. He'd told him nothing more than that. To say he hadn't been pleased when he'd first heard the news that Peter and Cheryl had hired Isabelle was an understatement of colossal proportions. She was a smart girl. They might as well have hung a sign around her neck that read I'M UNDER SURVEILLANCE. He'd felt sorry for her predicament, yes, but not sorry enough to want her around his own family.

His brother-in-law hadn't ended up as his riding's Member of Parliament by missing opportunities, however. He'd viewed the situation through a different filter.

"I checked her references, just like you asked. I had the RCMP run a background check, too. Hell, they even consulted Interpol, given how much she's traveled. When someone with excellent references, who's well-traveled and speaks four languages fluently, with no criminal record, lands on my doorstep needing a job when I need a nanny, I'm not slamming the door in her face. It's a win all around."

The RCMP and Interpol, and therefore Peter, didn't know she'd tried to sell her passport, though. Garrett had gotten an RCMP officer friend to pick her up at the airport on his own time, and take her passport from her, because he didn't want word to get out that CSIS had any interest in her. Neither body knew how deeply involved in organized crime her father, Marc Leon Beausejour, had become. He was only a small fish in a big, murky, cesspool of a pond, true, but hopefully, he'd lead CSIS to bigger catch.

Garrett's greatest concern right now was how much involvement Beausejour's daughter might have with organized crime too, and any potential danger she brought to his family. He'd searched Interpol's databases himself and found nothing on her. Peter's reports claimed she'd been an exemplary employee to date. The children liked her. She never went out alone, although distance and a lack of a driver's license no doubt accounted for that. She was quiet, and for the most part, did very little to draw attention to herself. When the children went to bed, she watched television or read books in her private suite. She had a preference for Russian literature. Cheryl had loaned her a laptop and Garrett had been monitoring her online activities for weeks. She'd contacted no one, not even friends. There appeared to be no significant other in her life.

So here he was, about to spend a month of vacation visiting his sister and digging for dirt, because Bangkok had been a bust. He'd found the Thai maintenance company that had been brokering the stolen weapons systems, but the only clear Canadian link appeared to be Isabelle's father, and he hadn't shown up for his last scheduled meeting with them. It was as if Beausejour had dropped off the face of the earth. If he was alive he had to be somewhere in Europe, where he could move across borders without having to present a passport. CSIS had already investigated the possibility he held more than one, and under different names, but no database photos had matched.

Isabelle's movements over the past five years had been easier to track because of her employment history, but before that, other than an occasional trip to Montreal, they were anyone's guess. Garrett was counting on at least some of her father's recent travels reflecting hers, especially around holidays and her birthday. Unfortunately, on her last birthday, she'd been in Bangkok.

Where her father hadn't shown.

He took the slender hand she offered him. "Well, well, Ms. Beausejour." He skated his eyes over her in a way that would have had his sister slapping him if she'd been here to see, but he was curious to see how she'd react. Maybe simple friendliness was the wrong approach to take with her if he wanted information. "What a pleasant surprise."

He meant the bikini, all skinny strings and tiny triangles of turquoise, and she had to know it, but if she did, she didn't let on.

"It's a very small world," she replied. She turned to Peter. "The children and I were about to go for a swim, but I think they've lost interest now. Would you like me to get them dressed?"

Peter lifted Chelsea, who'd been tugging on one of his fingers, into his arms, and kissed her plump little cheek before answering. "I've got some paperwork to do. I bet Uncle Garrett would love to go for a swim with them, though. Wouldn't he, guys?"

What Garrett would love more than anything was to spend time alone with Isabelle, figuring out what made her tick, but separating her from the children wasn't going to be easy. Peter knew that, so he'd handed him an excuse to stay close to her for the afternoon.

"Just let me go drop off my suitcase upstairs and change into my swim trunks," Garrett said.

He went to get his belongings from where he'd left them in the kitchen, then dragged his suitcase up two flights of stairs to the third floor. The Mansfords' house was a roomy, three-story dwelling on property owned by a third generation family farm in the middle of the province's largest dairy region. Peter had gone to law school, and then entered politics, while two of his older brothers ran the family business. Cheryl, Garrett's sister, worked in the nearby city of Halifax as a public defender with one of the law firms.

The third level of the house had two suites of rooms—one for long-term guests, like Garrett, and the other for any live-in help the Mansfords might hire, such as Isabelle. Each suite had a sitting room, bathroom, tiny kitchenette, and bedroom. The door to Isabelle's suite was closed.

He tried the knob. The door wasn't locked, nor had he expected it to be. He decided to have a quick look inside before she could hide anything she didn't want him to find. He propped his bag against the wall and opened the door.

The sitting room was neat and tidy, and identical to the one he'd be occupying, right down to the furnishings. There was a sofa, a flat screen TV, and DVD player. A closed laptop sat charging on the small glass coffee table. Next to it was a dog-eared copy of *Anna Karenina*. To the right of the room were the kitchenette and bathroom. Straight ahead was the bedroom.

Garrett poked around. Everything in the suite was neat and tidy. Isabelle didn't have many possessions, or if she did, she didn't carry them with her. He found her ancient canvas duffle bag in her closet, the one he'd helped her drag to the airport in Bangkok, along with a few articles of clothing on hangers. In the bathroom, her toiletries lined up neatly on the counter beside the sink. A clear plastic, zippered makeup bag had been tossed carelessly in the cupboard with the towels and spare rolls of toilet paper.

It was obvious Isabelle wasn't a hoarder. High maintenance, either. He tried to imagine his sisters surviving for more than a day with so few belongings. This visit, however, wasn't so much about unraveling secrets by prying into Isabelle's life as it was to win her trust, and hopefully track down her missing father.

He closed the door to her suite behind him and opened

his, heading straight to the bedroom. From its wide, double-hung windows, he had a view of the entire backyard. He dropped his suitcase on the king-sized bed and peered through the lace curtains.

It didn't take great observational powers to see that Isabelle was, indeed, good with the children. She stood on the side of the pool, her head tipped to one side, nodding occasionally, her dark ponytail sweeping one bare shoulder while she absorbed whatever Beth was explaining to her. He couldn't help but grin. It took a special kind of patience to listen to the bossy seven-year-old's long-winded and often roundabout stories.

She started to laugh at whatever Beth was saying to her. A wide, genuine smile transformed her face from average to something astonishing, revealing yet another one of her startling layers.

He let the curtain drop back into place.

No matter which way he tried to wrap his head around it, he couldn't figure out what her ultimate game was. Either she was innocent of any wrongdoing and her life totally sucked, or she was as deep in the cesspool as her father. He wished he believed it was the former, but he couldn't get past her attempt to sell that passport. She'd known what she was doing. If he hadn't caught on to what she was up to that night, she'd have succeeded. A part of him regretted not getting a chance to witness the performance she'd planned to put on at the Embassy.

He changed into his swim trunks and grabbed a pool towel from the linen closet in his bathroom, then headed downstairs and into the family room. He could hear Peter in his den at the front of the house, talking on the phone. He eased open the screen on the sliding patio door and walked to the edge of the pool.

Within seconds, he had what seemed like a horde of

screaming children hanging off his arms and legs, clinging like burrs.

"Did you guys multiply or something while I was inside?" he asked, grabbing Kiefer around the waist with one arm and flipping him upside down so that his chubby legs flailed in the air. "Because when I left, there were only three of you. Now there's got to be at least fifty."

"There's still only three of us," Chelsea assured him, her green eyes wide and serious. "Four, if we count Izzy."

He set Kiefer on his feet and glanced Isabelle's way. She was treading water in the deep end, sunlight glinting off her wet hair. He raised his eyebrows. "Izzy, huh?"

"Isabelle is a bit of a mouthful for young children. Peter and Cheryl have no problem pronouncing the unabridged version. You haven't had any trouble so far, either."

In other words, *Don't call me Izzy.*

He wasn't normally a difficult person. He got most of his informants to open up to him by being the "good" cop, not the bad one. Women usually liked him. He liked them, too. But there was something about Isabelle and her quiet, unflappable nature that made him want to shake all that calm. The last time he'd had the urge to be a jerk with a girl had been in the second grade. He'd had a huge crush on a cute blonde in the third row who didn't know he existed.

Since he wasn't eight years old anymore, and he couldn't put gum in her hair, that left calling her Izzy— but when the timing was right.

Right now was about having fun.

"Last one in the pool is a floater," Garrett said.

Isabelle watched him make a show of running for the diving board, giving the kids plenty of time to beat him into the water, then cannonball off the end. She scrambled for refuge in the shallow end, beating the peak of the tsunami he created by a matter of seconds. The girls clung to the sides of the pool, spluttering in the aftermath, having been buried in the crest.

Kiefer bobbed nearby, his chin bouncing in and out of the water. "*You* the floater, Uncle Garrett," he shouted.

"This explains so much." Isabelle started for the ladder. "Peter's going to have to refill the pool."

Since Garrett planned to play with the children, she might as well watch from the sidelines and enjoy the sunshine. Besides, he made her nervous. She worried too much about saying the wrong thing around him—which meant eventually, she would.

But she'd been thinking. If he was investigating her father, he might have information she sorely needed to hear. She'd never gone so many months without hearing from him. She had to know if he was at least still alive. She reminded herself daily that it would take some time for him to track her down. She didn't want to think about what it might mean if he never showed up, or what she would do if he didn't.

Somewhere, locked in her memories of her childhood, were tiny slivers of sadness attached to a mother whose face she could no longer remember. Once a year, until she was six or seven, she and her father would travel to a churchyard outside of Montreal and stand, hand in hand, at her grave. As much as she'd hated those trips, the thought of never knowing what had happened to her father was ten times worse.

If Garrett had information about him—any at all—she wanted to know.

She dried off with a towel and applied sunscreen, then settled into a padded lounge chair, determined to set her worries about both her father, and Garrett's sudden appearance, aside. She slid her sunglasses in place and closed her eyes, listening carefully to the children's voices so she'd know they were all accounted for. Even though she was certain their uncle could be trusted to watch them, she was the one who'd been hired as their caregiver. And she was fond of them.

A shadow passed over her, lingered for a few seconds, then she heard the scraping of the lounge chair next to hers being dragged across concrete, closer, and the creaks it made as it took a man's weight. Feigning sleep was tempting, but with no adult in the water to watch over the children, she didn't dare. She'd have to talk to Garrett eventually. It might as well be now.

She raised her lounge chair into an upright position. He was sitting on the edge of his, facing her. He'd combed his fingers through his short, damp hair, making it spike straight up in front. Dressed in navy board shorts, and in bare feet, she had to admit he wasn't quite as intimidating as he'd been in Bangkok. At least, not in the same way. He seemed much more relaxed.

She couldn't say the same about herself. In Bangkok, she'd been so wrapped up in her own situation she hadn't noticed much about him other than that he was a spy. She noticed more now. A killer smile spread all the way to his eyes, creating long, curved creases to embrace his mouth like a hug and reveal straight white teeth that must have cost his parents a fortune. The bent nose kept him from looking too pretty. It was his air of quiet confidence, however, that really set him apart. Garrett Downing was the kind of quick and efficient man who got things done— long before anyone noticed they needed doing. Isabelle would be lying if she said she didn't find him attractive. Most women would.

But he made her nervous. She struggled to think of something to say.

"I wanted to thank you again for your help in getting me out of Thailand," she said. "And for finding me work. The Mansfords are nice people."

"They are," he agreed. "But there's no need to thank me. You got this job all on your own."

If he hadn't asked Peter to hire her, then why was she here?

Disappointment, as dizzying as it was unexpected, hit her hard. She'd pinned too much hope on his interest in her father, believing that meant her father might still be alive. In fact, Garrett might not be CSIS at all. He might be exactly what he'd claimed to be in Thailand—a Canadian diplomat. One who had good observational skills, a conscience, and terrible taste in clothes. Behind the dark lenses she wore, she blinked back tears.

"Isabelle? Is something wrong?"

He was watching her, a slight frown in his eyes, trying to read her. She turned her head so she was facing the pool. She didn't want him or anyone else to know how afraid she was. "I was trying to figure out how long it will take me to save enough money to pay you back for the plane ticket and the hotel."

"And I told you before, there's no need. You never asked for my help. I gave it." Those perfect white teeth made another brief appearance. "In fact, if I remember correctly, I insisted."

Isabelle had met plenty of generous people, from all walks of life, over the years. She'd met an equal amount whose only interest was in helping themselves. She supposed she fit somewhere in between, along with the majority of the world. It didn't matter where he fit. She'd learned long ago that everyone's generosity had limitations—and showing signs of dependence or weakness was like pouring buckets of chum into shark-infested waters. Garrett had done too much for her to leave her with no obligation to him.

"I—" she began, when Kiefer called out to her.

"Izzy! Look at me!"

The three-year-old balanced precariously on one of the pool floats in the shallow end, his little arms out to the sides as he wobbled back and forth.

Isabelle shot to her feet at the same time as Garrett. "I see you *monsieur*, and you know the rules. No standing on pool toys. It is very dangerous."

She started forward, afraid he might fall and hit his head on the edge of the pool, but then Beth, always the bossy big sister, paddled up beside him, stood, and held up her hands.

"Off," she commanded. He leaped into her arms, taking them both under water. They resurfaced, giggling, and disaster was successfully averted.

Isabelle turned back to her chair and came forehead-to-chin with Garrett. He cupped her elbow to steady her, his fingers warm and firm. She had to tilt her head to look at him. He smelled of chlorine and sun-heated man, and as one solid thigh brushed against hers, her stomach made a queer little leap. She was thankful she wore sunglasses so he couldn't see her thoughts.

"The children like you," he said.

Isabelle found her voice, although it came out huskier than usual. "I like them, too."

He kept his hand on her elbow. The pad of his thumb shifted, sliding upward in an absent caress. "Do you also like living here?"

"The Mansfords are wonderful people."

"They are." The killer smile disappeared. "It means a lot to my sister to have someone reliable caring for her children. It does to me, too."

She got the message. He didn't trust her. While Isabelle understood, she resented him feeling the need to point it out.

"I only sell passports," she said. "The market for small children is too problematic. Speaking of passports," she added, as a new thought occurred to her, "when do I get mine back?" If he wasn't CSIS, then he had no reason to hold it. She hadn't committed any crime—or to more accurately state it, she hadn't completed committing one.

He made a show of surprise. "You mean you don't have it?"

She wasn't buying his act. "Your RCMP friend took it from me at the airport."

"You must be mistaken." Garrett dropped his hand from her arm and put a few paces between them. "My friend met you at the airport as a favor to me. The police would have no reason to take your passport from you."

She frowned at him. "This isn't funny."

"I'm not trying to be. Why do you need it, anyway? Are you planning a trip? Or don't Cheryl and Peter pay you enough and you're planning to sell it again?"

He was up to something. If he wouldn't return it, it was because he had a good reason not to. The only one she could think of was her father. Some of her earlier fear slid away. Hope eased into its place. "I want it because it's mine."

He studied her. She could almost see him choosing the right words.

"And I want to be able to sleep," he finally said, "knowing that my sister's new employee, who she trusts with her children, isn't going to sneak off in the middle of the night with the family silverware. Can you offer me a better guarantee that you won't?"

She couldn't.

"That's what I thought."

He strode off to rejoin his nieces and nephew in the water, leaving her with a better understanding of what the limits to his generosity toward her were.

Even if she wasn't as certain of his game.

CHAPTER THREE

GARRETT HAD MISSED THE mark on the fun part of his plan for getting to know Isabelle better. But she'd brought up the passport and Thailand, not him.

He leaned out of his lawn chair and took another beer from the cooler. Life, at the moment, was good. The fresh-mowed carpet of grass was soft and cool beneath his bare feet. Steak and smoked salmon were on the menu for dinner, and already, his mouth watered.

The men had taken charge of the barbecue, which mostly involved drinking beer while they waited for the grill to heat. Isabelle was in the kitchen tossing a salad. The girls were helping her. Kiefer played in a sandbox nearby, and Cheryl had called to say she'd be a few minutes late, but was bringing dessert. He'd bet money it was chocolate cheesecake. That was his favorite.

At the end of the day, there was nothing Garrett liked better than kicking back and relaxing in the countryside with his sister and her family. Cheryl and Peter both had busy careers, but they knew what was important in life. Their kids came first.

"Now do you believe me?" Peter asked, taking a swig of his beer. "She's completely normal."

"Yeah?" Garrett twisted the cap off his bottle and tossed it onto the glass-and-wrought-iron table with the others. Do you think it's completely normal that a twenty-four-year old woman has absolutely no friends or family to speak of?"

"No," Peter said. "But I do think it's none of my business. We both know not everyone in the world was raised by June and Ward Cleaver."

"True. But no one normal goes through life without making friends. She's a pretty woman. Why isn't there a boyfriend somewhere?"

"You're not a bad-looking guy. Why no girlfriend?"

"Who says there isn't?"

"Is there?"

"No," Garrett admitted. "Women usually take issue with my lifestyle at some point."

Peter leaned back in his lawn chair, stretching his legs. "I can't imagine why a woman would object to you heading off for parts unknown, for months at a time, without any explanation."

"I know. Unreasonable, right?" Garrett picked at the bottle's label with his thumbnail. "Does she seem at all worried to you? Upset about anything?"

"Not in the least."

That wasn't the impression Garrett had received earlier. When he'd told her she'd gotten this job on her own, rather than pleased, she'd almost seemed devastated. Then, when he'd refused to give back her passport, she'd looked relieved. Something worried her. Something big. But he'd be damned if he could figure out what.

Good cop, he reminded himself. He'd missed the mark on that today, too.

"Any ideas on ways I can spend time with her without the rugrats underfoot?" Garrett asked. "I mean, I love them, you know I do. But I've got to work while I'm here."

Peter was the only one in the family who could say for certain that Garrett was with CSIS, and only because CSIS was accountable to various government departments, one of which Peter watchdogged. He had no idea what Garrett's work entailed, however, and knew better than to ask.

Peter frowned at his beer. "She runs before Cheryl leaves for the city in the mornings, and I haven't been crazy about her going alone. For someone who's lived in Africa, she doesn't seem to have a good grasp of the potential for danger from wild animals. We've had coyotes around the farm. You could start running with her. I have a pair of shoes still in the box you can use. I'll tell her I insist, if you want."

More news he didn't like. He'd seen a few Eastern coyotes, so he understood Peter's concern, and it was valid. Part wolf, they could grow to weigh seventy-five pounds or more. While most were opportunists and scavengers, like their Western coyote cousins, too many had exhibited wolf-like hunting behavior to be dismissed as harmless. There'd been at least one death in the province attributed to them. "Why haven't you been running with her if it isn't safe?"

"I haven't been home very much since she's been here. When I am, she's a little jumpy around me," Peter said. "I didn't want to push the issue. A few of the guys on the farm have taken dogs into the woods and they haven't found any dens, so it's not a huge worry. Just a concern."

The thought of running, especially early in the morning, held little appeal. Given a choice, Garrett would take weightlifting and swimming. Running wouldn't give them much time to talk, but since Isabelle wasn't proving to be much of a talker anyway, he could use the opportunity to build trust instead. It was better than nothing. "Please tell me she isn't a long-distance marathoner."

Peter tipped his beer bottle at him, a faint smirk on his face. "Let's just say if it comes to a race, she's not the one who's going to have to worry about coyotes."

"Hey there, little brother!"

Garrett half turned at the interruption. Cheryl tottered across the grass toward him, a glass of red wine held high in one hand. He tried not to laugh. She hadn't changed out of her office clothes yet, and crossing the lawn in those high heels had to be tricky.

Thirty-seven years old, she was as pretty and bubbly as ever. Her eyes were the same color as his, and so was her hair, although she'd added blonde highlights to hers. No one who met them had ever missed the fact they were siblings, but where Garrett was broad and muscular, she was petite, almost delicate—living proof that appearances could be deceiving. According to the papers she was a shark in the courtroom, and he had more than thirty years' worth of firsthand experience as to how determined she could be. It was no secret in the family as to who her eldest daughter got her bossiness from.

Man, he loved her.

So did her husband. Peter got to her first, lifting the glass from her hand and giving her a kiss that had Garrett shaking his head. "Cut it out, you two. There are children present. Not to mention, I may lose my lunch."

"You're just jealous that I found someone awesome and you haven't." Cheryl held out her arms to him. Gold bangles jingled on one slim wrist. "Come here, you big, spoiled baby. I bought you a chocolate cheesecake for dessert."

"I knew you would, so if I'm spoiled, it's all thanks to you."

As he hugged his sister, Garrett caught a glimpse of Isabelle, standing on the deck with a platter of steaks for the barbecue in her hands. She'd changed from the bikini into a short, tie-dyed, yellow silk dress that flowed like water over her curves. He'd seen similar dresses at the roadside markets throughout Southeast Asia. While simple in style, the colorful fabric and foreign cut, combined with her natural, light-olive complexion and dark eyes, gave her an exotic air. He couldn't figure out why his first impression of her had been so far off base. She wasn't plain.

Not at all.

But it was the wistful expression on her face, there for only a second, that gave him pause. From everything she'd said, and what he'd been able to learn, except for an irresponsible father who'd dragged her all over the world, she had no one. He had sisters, parents, grandparents, aunts, uncles, cousins... The list went on. He couldn't imagine a life not filled with family.

She carried the platter to the barbecue and would have slipped quietly back into the house without drawing attention to herself if Peter hadn't stopped her. "You're off the clock, Isabelle. Garrett's cooking the steak and I've got the salmon. Cheryl wants to spend time with the kids. Why don't you go pour yourself a glass of wine and join us?"

"Just let me get rid of my pantyhose first," Cheryl said to her. "Then you and I can let the hunters show us gatherers how real men cook meat. We'll be right back," she called over her shoulder, dragging Isabelle to the house along with her. "Don't drink my wine."

"I wouldn't dare." Peter kept a cautious eye on his

wife's back as he took a long swig from her glass, then set it on the table beside the barbecue. "What?" he demanded in response to Garrett's raised eyebrow. "I'm telling her you drank it."

"Thanks a lot. My piece of cheesecake just got cut in half."

Thirty minutes later, they sat down to dinner at the table outdoors.

Throughout the meal, Garrett studied Isabelle. She helped cut Chelsea's meat for her, and mopped up the trickle of milk Kiefer spilled with one of the paper napkins, but other than comments to the children, she had little to say. It wasn't that she was shy around Peter and Cheryl. Him either, for that matter. She simply seemed to prefer soaking up the family dynamics without interfering in them. She was an observer. The intelligence officer in Garrett wondered how much of her father's activities someone like Isabelle might have absorbed, and if he could somehow make use of it.

"Peter tells me you run in the mornings," he said to her.

She paused in the process of lifting a forkful of salad to her mouth, then lowered the untouched food to her plate. She rested the stainless steel shaft of the fork on the table and reached for her wine.

"I do." Her eyes assessed him over the rim of the glass as she took a sip, no doubt well aware of where he was headed with this topic of conversation. "Are you a runner?"

He settled back, prepared for an argument and rather looking forward to one. He couldn't say why, but he enjoyed getting a rise out of her. "Used to be. I thought I'd get back into it. A desk job has made me soft."

"You're welcome to join me," she said. "I start at 5:30 a.m. Tomorrow is my six and a half mile run."

She'd issued a challenge. He could see it in her eyes. There was no way he could manage that kind of run starting out and she knew it. He'd be damned if he let her win this, however.

"I'd end up in a coma if I tried that," he said. "But I hate to turn down an invitation to be your workout buddy. Tell you what. I'll ride a bike with you on your long-distance days and at least get in some exercise, then run the shorter distance days."

She retrieved her fork and ate the mouthful of salad. If her brain were a steam engine smoke would be rolling out of her ears, she was thinking so hard about ways to say no. Garrett prepared for the next obstacle she planned to throw at him. He enjoyed a good challenge.

Instead, she surprised him.

"I'd like that." She smiled. "Afterward, you can join me for yoga. Proper stretching is so important. It's also good for strengthening the mind. We wouldn't want you to hurt yourself." She raised her glass to him in a mini salute. Her eyes sparkled. "Being workout buddies will be fun. Thank you for suggesting it."

"Great idea," Peter said to him. "Good luck with your quest for inner peace."

"Yes, great idea," Cheryl echoed. The frown pinching her brow warned Garrett she thought it was anything but. She'd have a few things to say about it when she got him alone. He hated running and she knew it.

The thought of yoga was worse. Guys didn't do yoga. If he tried to find an excuse to avoid it, however, he lost an opportunity to spend alone time with Isabelle. If he said yes, his sister was going to think he was pursuing her. She'd be right, but for the wrong reasons. "I'm good with the whole stretching thing, but I'll pass on the yoga."

"Why?" Isabelle asked.

Cheryl's gaze sharpened into her courtroom stare. "Yes, Garrett, why?" Her eyes shifted to the children, who were listening to the adult exchange with open curiosity. "Because I'm sure you don't mean to imply that there's anything wrong with men practicing yoga."

Damn it. He'd forgotten there were kids at the table. "No, no, not at all." He scrambled to think of a believable excuse that wouldn't dig him in deeper. "I'm just not very flexible."

"Don't worry," Isabelle assured him. "Yoga's great for improving flexibility. I'll come up with a simple routine to get you started."

"Make sure it involves flexing his mind, too," Cheryl said to her. "His has gotten a little flabby."

"Can a brain get fat?" Beth interrupted, her eyes wide and curious.

"Seems your Uncle Garrett's can," Peter said, which sparked another scolding from his wife.

Garrett's eyes met Isabelle's across the table. She smiled at him, and it was the merriment in her expression that did him in. He had to smile back, although his was more rueful. He could admit it. She was as clever as she was pretty, and she'd just outplayed him.

He'd underestimated her.

On so many levels.

"I didn't realize you and Garrett had met in Thailand," Cheryl said.

And Isabelle hadn't realized that Cheryl didn't know, because her husband definitely did.

The two women were in the kitchen, loading the

dishwasher and putting leftovers away. The men were getting the children into their pajamas and brushing their teeth. The unspoken question in Cheryl's voice said she'd noticed her brother's unusual interest in her children's new nanny and had drawn the wrong conclusion.

The possibility of Garrett being attracted to someone like Isabelle was laughable. Yes, she'd seen the way he looked at her when she was wearing a bikini, and again when she'd shown up to dinner in a short summer dress. She hadn't been trying to make an impression on him. She'd been living in a third world country with a hot climate and lightweight clothes were all she owned these days. The local dresses were pretty, cheap, and easy to pack. Everything before she'd left for Thailand had gone to a consignment store, as it invariably did when she and her father changed locations. Either she sold what she had no use for, or she gave it to charity.

She dropped a handful of rinsed flatware into the tray, then reached for the liquid detergent. Cheryl was a lawyer. Not to mention, Isabelle discovered that having the Mansfords' good opinion of her mattered.

She stuck to the truth when she answered the question. "I'd found myself in a bad situation in Bangkok. I was stranded and had no money. Garrett was working at the Embassy and bought me a plane ticket home."

"And then he asked Peter to give you a job," Cheryl said, filling in what she saw as the blanks, and Isabelle didn't correct her. "Garrett likes helping people. He's always been that way. That's why he chose to be a government program officer when our parents would have rather he went into the family automotive business."

She sounded so proud of him.

"Is that what he is? A government program officer? What do they do?"

"Lots of things, but in Garrett's case, he travels to foreign countries to work with the embassies. He transfers between different departments all the time. Sometimes he helps people immigrate to Canada. Sometimes he organizes disaster relief." Cheryl fastened cling wrap over the remains of the cheesecake and slid it into the stainless steel fridge. She closed the door with her hip. "When he was in Bangkok, he was with the Canadian Defence attaché's office. A Defence attaché helps foreign military contractors who want to do business with the Canadian government, and Canadian contractors looking to do business in foreign countries. His travel and work keep him too busy, though. Other than the odd week here and there, I don't think he's taken a real vacation in the last five years."

Isabelle punched the settings on the dishwasher. It hummed to life. Maybe Garrett wasn't CSIS. If not, that was both good and bad. While he might not have information on her father, he could still be in a position to help her find out what had happened to him.

But she didn't trust Garrett enough to ask. She didn't dare. He showed far too much interest in her. And she simply wasn't that special. That Defence attaché connection bothered her, too. As an international security management specialist, her father sometimes did business with military contractors in foreign countries, although mostly in Eastern Europe. He'd only been planning to go to Thailand to meet up with her. He had no business there.

As far as you know, a tiny voice whispered.

And Cheryl said Garrett rarely took a vacation. That made the timing of this one particularly suspicious.

"Isabelle?" Cheryl was saying. "Something wrong?"

"I've got a bit of a headache." She rubbed her forehead. "If you don't mind, I'm going to head to my room for the rest of the evening. I'll leave you to your family time. You haven't seen your brother in a while."

"As long as you're with us, you're part of the family. You don't need to spend your evenings alone," Cheryl reminded her.

"Thank you." Isabelle appreciated the kind words even though she didn't believe them. She didn't want to impose on the Mansfords, or encourage them, either. She was here for the summer. She'd never stayed in one place long enough to become part of anything so it was always easier on everyone, especially the children, not to become too attached.

She stopped at the second floor to wish the children good night, then went to her suite on the third. She curled into the sofa in front of the television and flipped open the laptop. She surfed a few of the online shopping websites, looking at shoes, then went to etsy.com.

Nothing. No message from her father.

Where are you, Papa?

She tapped her finger on the keypad. Then she looked up the Canadian Security Intelligence Service Act. Whitewashed and boring. She moved on to her favorite ebookstores before finally closing the laptop, then read for a few hours before turning out the light and heading to bed. Five thirty would come soon enough. She hadn't yet heard Garrett come upstairs, and wondered if he'd be awake in time for their run.

If not, she had no plans to wait for him.

As Isabelle stepped into the hall the next morning, she bumped into Garrett outside her door. He was leaning against the wall, obviously waiting for her. She bit back a scream, pressing a hand to her pounding chest, not wanting to wake the entire house.

"You nearly gave me a heart attack."

"Sorry."

He looked anything but.

He wore a gray cotton T-shirt, with DALHOUSIE UNIVERSITY stenciled in black and gold letters across the front, and a black pair of track shorts. His pristine white running shoes appeared to be straight out of the box—the brand, top of the line. While his hair looked as if he'd just crawled out of bed, he managed to come across as rumpled and sexy, not sloppy. He'd said he preferred weightlifting to running, and it showed in the heavy muscles of his shoulders and thighs, and the thickness of his chest.

She felt drab standing beside him. Her sports bra and pink tank top were ancient and frayed at the seams. She'd gotten her racing shorts at a thrift shop five years ago when she and her father were living in Amsterdam. Her running shoes, however, she never scrimped on. She'd bought a few quality pairs in Asia because they'd been cheap. She'd scraped her straight hair into its usual high ponytail. The tip tickled the bare skin between her shoulders, just above the back of her sports bra.

"I thought you were biking this morning, not running," she said.

A crooked smile curled the corners of his mouth. "I am. But I might try running the last mile. You should be tired enough by then for me to keep up." He stepped out of her way and gestured for her to go ahead of him to the stairs.

Isabelle remained where she was. "This isn't your sport, so why are you doing this?"

"To be honest? Because Peter asked me to. He seemed concerned about coyotes."

She held up her wrist. A red lifeguard whistle dangled from a plastic cord. "I'm safe. If this can clear a pool of a hundred screaming children, a coyote's ears are going to ring."

He started to laugh, the sound so low and sexy that heat pooled in her belly. "Seriously? You think a whistle's going to stop something that's planning to eat you?"

She had. Now, she wasn't so sure. "When's the last time someone's been eaten by a coyote around here?"

"You don't need to worry about the last person. You need to worry about the next." He turned more serious. "I agree the odds are low, but it's happened. These are wolf crosses, therefore unpredictable, and you, Isabelle Beausejour, have a complete disregard for danger even when it's staring you in the face. I'm perfectly happy to go running with you, or biking, in this particular instance, to make sure you're okay."

She tried to read him, to see if he was telling the truth or trying to scare her. Peter had told her several times she should be careful, especially near the stretches of woodland, so Garrett's explanation made sense. But despite what he might think, she didn't have a disregard for danger at all. In fact, when she was around him, the needle on her hazard meter flipped straight to the red zone. That same sense of self-preservation warned there was more to this sudden desire of his to start running again. He was already fit.

Practicality intervened. It said to use this opportunity to her advantage. To find out what he knew about her father, if anything, or at the very least, what he wanted to know. There was no reason she couldn't have a little fun with it, too.

"Are we still on for yoga?" she asked.

He made a face. "My sister will have my head if I don't at least give it a try. Thanks for that, by the way. I plan to get even."

It was her turn to smile. "You'll love it. I promise."

He went very still. His expression shifted, growing more intense, taking on the alertness she'd noticed in Bangkok that said he was mentally recording every minute detail about her. She'd done something. Said something. What?

"You have a beautiful smile. You should use it more often," he said.

No flippant response came to mind. Most men never noticed her smile, or if they did, found nothing about it worth commenting on. She'd had boyfriends, true, although they'd been just that—boys, with no interest in anything but fun—as transient as she was, and too young to think of the future.

Garrett was no boy. This was danger, a kind she wasn't familiar with, and as he said, it was staring her straight in the face.

The hall was narrow, without a lot of room, and growing smaller by the moment. Minimal light filtered in from the window at the far end. She made a move to slide past him. A hand shot up. It hit the wall beside her head, blocking the way. His eyes, a warm, heated hazel, met hers.

"I'm sorry. That was intended as a compliment. I didn't mean to make you uncomfortable."

"You didn't."

He hadn't. Not in a way she could object to, or begin to articulate, without feeling like a foolish *naïf*.

His eyes dropped to her lips. Seconds later, his mouth covered hers. Sparks of desire showered through her, leaving her lightheaded and breathless. His hand fell to her hip. One of his knees slid between her thighs, pressing her back against the wall. The tip of his tongue brushed her lips. Her fingers gripped the front of his T-shirt, whether to make closer contact and deepen the kiss, or to stay on her feet, she couldn't be sure.

He pulled back, not saying anything, simply watching her face, a slight frown on his as if he, too, were puzzled by his actions. She untangled her fingers from the soft fabric of his shirt, digging deep for the calm she normally hid herself in, but he was standing too close. She could feel the movement of each muscle, and each inhale and exhale as he breathed. She didn't want him to know how much he'd surprised her, or how much she'd enjoyed that kiss. She couldn't believe it, herself.

"What was that for?" she asked. She sounded so normal, when in reality, chaos swelled and alarm bells rang.

"Do I need a reason to kiss a pretty woman?"

Yes. And his was one he'd no doubt carefully considered. She'd do well not to forget that. Whether or not he was CSIS, he wasn't the type of man to be interested in a woman like her. Not in his sister's home. Not near her impressionable young children. Isabelle had no education. No impeccable family. Therefore, he wanted something.

So did she. Her father might not be perfect, but she loved him. She needed to know he was safe.

She smoothed the front of Garrett's shirt with the palms of her hands. Her heart settled back to its usual rhythm. She'd always prided herself on her reserve and ability to remain calm in most situations. She could resist a man who was playing games with her.

"We're going to be late," she said.

His eyes filled with humor. "We can't have that happen."

He was laughing at her. He made no comment about her avoiding his question, however. Instead, he stepped out of the way so she could pass by.

CHAPTER FOUR

GARRETT GAVE HER CREDIT. It didn't look like he was going to get anywhere with her the old-fashioned way. Kissing her—flirting—wasn't the right approach.

He was willing to give it another shot though, just to be sure.

He wheeled Peter's ancient fifteen-speed bicycle out of the garage attached to the house and walked it down the driveway. The sun had only half-cleared the cloudless horizon as of yet, and the early morning air was cool and fresh, perfect for running. Dew sparkled on the front lawn. A tiny breath of wind ruffled the silver leaves on the poplars. In the distance, beyond a low hill, the muted roar of machinery told him the farm was already awake and at work.

Isabelle waited for him on the shoulder of the road, swinging her arms, all long, lean muscle and feminine curves.

He liked her, he discovered. The quiet, solid, comforting calmness of her. The unembellished prettiness and subtle sense of humor. The fearlessness. No, not so much fearlessness, as confidence and independence. Sandwiched smack in the middle of it all, however, was a thin layer of vulnerability. Every once in a while, when she thought no one was looking, he'd catch tiny sparkles of it, like bits of broken glass embedded in steel. She brought out every male instinct he owned—a disquieting discovery, because he'd have thought honesty would carry more weight with him.

He reminded his instincts that he'd caught her red-handed trying to sell her passport.

In order to survive, they whispered back.

At dinner last night, his sister had noticed his interest as more than casual curiosity and taken him aside to issue a warning. *"Don't screw around with Isabelle, Garrett. I mean it. The kids like her and so do I. Peter does, too."*

So it was unanimous. Everyone liked her. The trouble was, it was too easy to be taken in by conmen—or conwomen. Most people liked them. Garrett had met quite a few, and while Isabelle didn't have the same kind of charisma, she had…something, and he wasn't immune to it, either.

"Ready?" he asked her, straddling the bicycle and testing the hand brakes. They were stiff but secure. Kind of like his knees.

She nodded, then started out in long, easy strides, with all the fluid gracefulness of an experienced runner. Garrett followed along beside her, careful to let her set the pace and not push her too hard.

"How long have you been running?" he asked.

"Fourteen years."

Since she was ten. He hated running, so that boggled the mind. "Why so young?"

She didn't turn her head to look at him, and kept her words to a minimum, conserving her breath. "Something my father and I could do together."

"Does your father still run, too?"

"Yes."

Garrett filed that piece of information away. It might or might not prove useful later on. Every little bit helped.

Any more attempts at conversation died at the first hill. He hadn't realized how many there were around here. For a long time the only sounds came from the humming of the bicycle tires, Isabelle's measured breathing, the slap of her shoes' rubber soles against asphalt, and the occasional car passing by.

Garrett dropped behind her so he could watch her run, purely for pleasure. She held her back straight, her bent elbows chest high. The straight length of chestnut-colored ponytail danced rhythmically back and forth between her shoulder blades as her arms pumped. Her shorts, thin and worn with washings and age, clung to rounded buttocks and exposed a long length of upper thigh. Again, there was no single, standout feature about her that made him enjoy watching her so much. She was beautiful for her simplicity, a perfect daisy, rather than an ornamental rose.

They reached the halfway point in her run and turned toward home. Traffic had begun to pick up as the neighbors, most of whom commuted to the city, began heading for work. By now, Garrett's thigh muscles were screaming and his butt was sore. It had been a long time since he'd ridden a bicycle—longer, even, than his last run.

When he judged they were almost a mile from the house he put on a burst of speed to get ahead of her, then dismounted and propped the bicycle in the bushes surrounding an oak tree so he could come back for it later. He fell into step beside her when she caught up.

She'd maintained a steady pace from the beginning, but now she slowed.

"You sure about this?" she asked him, a challenge in her eyes.

"Hell, no. But if I sit on that bike any longer, I'll be eating my meals standing up for the rest of the week."

She smiled at that, and without further comment, refocused her attention on the road.

He wouldn't claim running a mile was easy, especially not after biking more than five already, but five minutes in, he began to have faith he might make it. They'd almost reached the driveway, and his hopes remained high, when his hamstring seized. He stumbled, drawing up short, then bent at the waist with his leg extended as he tried to stretch it out.

Isabelle stopped when she realized he was no longer beside her, turned around, and jogged back. "Did you pull a muscle?"

"Tendon, I think." He had no intention of telling her how bad it hurt—he was no sissy—but his sweating could no longer be blamed on either exercise or the rising heat.

Her cocoa-brown eyes, soft and rich, shimmered with concern. "See if you can walk it out. Here. Let me help."

Before he could refuse, she'd slipped her arm around his waist and draped his over her shoulders. With her snuggled against him, he lost all interest in arguing the matter.

He limped as far as the front lawn and eyed the door of the house. It looked ten miles away, but he figured he could make it under his own steam as long as he didn't stop moving. The last thing he wanted was for Cheryl or Peter to catch him like this. He'd never hear the end of it.

"The leg's much better now," he lied. "A hot shower and I'll be good as new."

He was reluctant to let go of her, however. He still had his arm around her, and her expression as she peered up at him from beneath it said she wasn't buying whatever he was trying to sell.

He wanted to kiss her again.

"Lie on the grass and I'll help you stretch it first. Then you can shower," she said.

All of which brought up vivid images of much more than kissing.

A car drove past. The driver waved to them. They waved back.

"Not a chance," Garrett replied. "Not out here for the whole world to see."

Her lips pressed together in a way that suggested she was trying hard not to laugh, but when she spoke, she sounded sympathetic. "You aren't the first person to ever get a muscle cramp or pulled tendon from exercise, but we could go around the back of the house, if you'd prefer. Can you make it that far?"

He would if it killed him.

When they reached the back yard, Garrett collapsed on the grass. "If you've got suggestions for stretching it out, I'm willing to listen."

She knelt beside him. "Give me your foot." He lifted it with a groan. She scooted over a few inches so that her hip touched the inside of his sound leg. She placed one hand under the calf of the sore leg, below his knee, the other on his thigh above it, so that the sole of his shoe rested against the flat front of her shoulder. "Now press your foot into me."

As he did, she rubbed the stiff muscles of his thigh and calf with strong fingers. He groaned again, this time with pleasure. It felt amazing.

He watched her face as she worked. Long lashes shielded her thoughts from him. A slight frown of concentration furrowed a vee between her brows. A thin sheen of perspiration coated her throat and upper chest, above the tank top and sports bra. His thoughts wandered in a far more dangerous direction. A little to the south.

She tucked her hand under the heel of his shoe and forced his leg upward, stretching the hamstring. "Any better?" she asked.

"Much." He rested the back of his head on clasped hands, gazing up at her. "You're full of all kinds of surprising talents. You could do this for a living."

"Believe it or not, I like looking after children more than massaging men's thighs."

She let go of his foot. He planted it on the ground beside her, fencing her in between his bent knees. She sat back on her heels, but she didn't stand up or push him away. He trailed the tips of his fingers up the length of her bare thigh to play with the hem of her shorts, telling himself he only wanted to see how far he could push her level of comfort.

He got no more reaction than he had the day before, when he'd admired her in that bikini, or this morning, when he'd kissed her. She showed no outrage or discomfort. No interest, either. She gave no outward indication she was bothered by him.

Not as much as he was by her.

Yet he didn't believe she was unaffected. If she were, she wouldn't bother hiding her responses so well.

"You can't look after other people's children forever, or keep traveling from country to country, taking low-end jobs," he said, trying a different tactic. "Kids grow up and move on. What do you want to do with the rest of your life? Any burning desires?"

"Cheryl says you're a government program officer, and that you travel a lot," Isabelle countered. "Does your work make you happy? Does it matter to you what the pay is?"

Those were good questions. He wasn't certain he had any answers. Being a program officer was part of his cover. It was what he told people he did, and in fact, he quite often carried out the duties assigned to the position. He liked his work with CSIS too, and while the money was good, it wasn't the reason he'd accepted the job. Part of its appeal was in serving his country, although the thrill of the chase—and putting together pieces of a puzzle that led to an arrest and conviction—were what mattered the most. He also liked pushing limits.

But he wouldn't do any of it for free. Bills had to be paid. A man had to eat. He could guarantee her father wasn't moving stolen military property out of the goodness of his heart either.

He splayed his hand against the warmth of her thigh. He was going way too far now, but she had such smooth skin—soft—yet underneath, it was solid, sleek muscle. He wondered how she'd reacted when her employer in Thailand cornered her in the garden. If she'd been as cool about it as she'd been when he kissed her.

He didn't like the mental comparison.

"Were you happy when I found you in Bangkok?" he asked.

It was a jerk thing to say. A spark of emotion flared in her eyes, then was gone. She lifted his hand from her thigh, not answering his question. Pressing her palms to his knees, she pushed to her feet.

"You are not finished stretching, *monsieur*. *Maintenant*. We've only got about fifteen minutes before I have to prepare breakfast."

He had his tell. Her English was impeccable, and spoken like a native Anglophone, yet she became more French—and very brisk—when she was rattled. He'd noticed it in Bangkok, and again when she dealt with the children in the pool yesterday, particularly Kiefer. They knew when she meant business.

He blew out a loud sigh. "I was hoping you'd forget." He held up a hand and she took it, steadying him as he stood. He tested the leg. The hamstring really did feel better. "Let's get this over with."

She was unsympathetic as she showed him how to hold a few simple yoga poses. "I won't make you practice the breathing this time. We'll work on that another day."

As he made half-hearted attempts at the stretches, hoping no one in the house—meaning Peter—could see him, he watched her move through her own routine. Downward dog was one he recognized. From his angle and perspective, and level of appreciation, the pose was misnamed. It should have a much sexier label. While she made it look easy, there was no way his bulkier body would ever be as graceful at this as hers. He was equally certain no one was going to be seeing his ass in that same position.

He tried to distract himself from the sight of hers by tallying up what he knew about her to add to his case file. She was smart, athletic, and unmotivated by money. At least, so she claimed. She wasn't easily intimidated, and would do what she believed necessary in order to survive. Bangkok had proved that to him.

Then he recalled what she'd said to him earlier. How she'd taken up running because it was something she could do with her father. In Bangkok, she'd told him that she and her father were no longer as close as they once were—that when he wanted to see her, he found her.

The light bulb came on. Satisfaction hummed through him. That didn't mean they were estranged. Isabelle wasn't reaching out to her father because she really didn't know where he was.

Which meant Beausejour would be contacting her. But how?

Isabelle had scrambled eggs, toast, and fresh fruit waiting on the kitchen table by the time Cheryl, Peter, and the children came downstairs.

Garrett had already gone for his shower. While the family ate, she ran upstairs to take hers.

The next few weeks would be long ones. She didn't know for sure what he hoped to achieve with the kisses, light touches, and admiring glances, but her thoughts and emotions tangled into all sorts of complicated knots when it came to him. He interested her. Excited her.

Annoyed her.

She should avoid him.

Before she got in the shower, out of habit, she opened the laptop and went to etsy.com. She browsed a few items.

And there it was. The message from her father that she'd been waiting for, hidden in a site for handcrafted gold rings. Her breath caught as she clicked on the link and discovered that the ring she chose was only available through backorder. The world began to spin. She sank to the floor, resting her cheek on bent knees.

Backorder meant she couldn't contact him unless there was an extreme emergency, which in turn, meant he'd gone into hiding. At least now she knew he was alive.

It didn't lessen her fear that he might not be for much longer. Garrett was right when he'd said she couldn't continue to live this way. The important question wasn't whether or not she'd been happy in Bangkok, however. It was if she was happy now. She wasn't. She had no choice other than to continue to wait for her father.

Peter had offered her this position for the summer, however. At best, she had another six weeks before the girls started school and Kiefer went back to daycare. If her father didn't resurface by then, she'd have a limited amount of money in her pocket and nowhere to go.

Without her passport, she wouldn't be going very far.

For a long time, she didn't move. Then, she made her way to the shower. By the time she got dressed and returned to the kitchen, Garrett was alone at the breakfast table, drinking coffee. Cheryl and Peter had already left for the city. She could hear the children in the playroom, watching television.

Her chest tightened at the sight of him. It was important he not realize anything was wrong, for her father's sake if not her own. He read her far too easily.

He held up a set of car keys.

"We're taking the kids sightseeing today," he said. "Peter tells me you don't drive, which means I get to chauffeur."

A girlfriend in South Africa had taught her how to drive an ancient field truck with a stick shift when they were thirteen or fourteen, but that was a long time ago, and besides, she didn't know any Canadian rules of the road. She'd been putting off learning, hoping to hear from her father, not knowing for certain how long she'd be here. She had no real reason to procrastinate anymore. Her stay in Canada could be indefinite.

She tried to summon enthusiasm. "I'm planning to get my license. I've got a copy of the learner's handbook and I've been studying it."

She must have sounded defensive because the hint of a smile, understanding and sincere, seeped into his hazel eyes. "It's not a criticism, Isabelle. I told Peter I'd give you a few lessons while I'm here." The smile spread to his lips, taking on a slight tinge of mischief. "You know. As payback for the yoga instruction."

"It's so hard to resist such a kind, generous offer when you put it like that." She slid into a chair and reached for the bowl of strawberries, a banana, and a slice of fresh bread, which she dropped in the toaster. The looks he gave her thawed a layer of the fear numbing her heart, making it difficult to remember this was no more than a game to him. "Where would you like to go sightseeing?"

They discussed a few options before settling on a drive to the beach. "We could go to the city another day," Garrett suggested. "Maybe Cheryl will be able to join us, and you ladies can shop while the kids and I go bowling or to a movie."

"I'm not much of a shopper." Certainly not at the stores his sister would frequent. She had to save her money for the next emergency she didn't doubt would be coming. She'd been left high and dry in Bangkok by one set of employers she'd trusted. That wasn't happening again.

His raised eyebrows said he didn't believe her about the shopping, but he let it pass. "What do you like to do for fun, then? Other than running. And yoga. You'll never convince me anyone enjoys that, by the way. A lobotomy would be a better way to empty your head."

The comparison made her laugh. Whether this was a game to him or not, Garrett was going out of his way to be charming. It was nice. She spent a lot of her time as an au pair trying not to intrude on her employers' family life, and sometimes, it got lonely. She didn't often have anyone to share a laugh with. Troubles, either.

She wished she could trust him.

"I don't think the purpose of yoga is to empty your

head quite so literally," she said, "but for fun, I like to see how other people live."

Garrett's gaze latched onto hers. "Considering all the exotic places you've been, Nova Scotia must seem dull."

"You've traveled a lot, too," she pointed out, "so you should understand that Nova Scotia is as exotic as any other place in the world. It all depends on what you're used to, and I've never seen the Atlantic Ocean before. Montreal's the extent of my knowledge of Canada." She finished her toast and drank the last of her juice. She'd love to know if the things Cheryl had told her about him and his work were the truth. She really wanted them to be. It had been too long since she'd had anyone she could confide in. "I notice you didn't invite yourself along on this shopping trip you proposed. So what do you like to do for fun when you're on vacation? Or are you always working?"

Holding the mug in both hands, he took a sip of his coffee. "I like to take beautiful women to the beach so they can see the Atlantic Ocean."

Which told her nothing of value, although it did bring another smile to her face. "Then I guess this is your lucky day. There'll be three of us, with a handsome young gentleman thrown in as a bonus." She gathered her dirty dishes and carried them to the dishwasher. "Give me half an hour to pack a lunch and get the children ready."

"You take care of the children. I'll finish my coffee and make sandwiches."

They were on the road within an hour.

The Mansfords had a minivan they used for family road trips. Isabelle found the sight of Garrett sitting behind its wheel, with three young children bickering among themselves in the back, ludicrous—and therefore, entertaining. On the surface, it was difficult to reconcile this man with the one who'd grabbed her wrist in Bangkok, foiling her attempt to sell her passport. There, he'd been all business. Here, he was much more approachable. Likeable. He made her smile. She was seeing two sides to him. She had no idea which one was real.

"What's so funny?" he asked as he backed the van out of the driveway.

"A minivan doesn't impress me as your usual type of transportation."

"No?" An eyebrow went up. "What is my type, then?"

She pretended to give it some thought. "The gray car James Bond drives in the movie Casino Royale, perhaps."

"An Aston Martin?"

"A spy car," she corrected him. "What do Canadian spies drive?"

He didn't miss a beat. "Probably something more economical. And with better mileage. I hear in Toronto, they ride the Go trains." He slid a sly glance at her from the corner of his eye. "In Bangkok, I bet they hire tuk-tuks."

"Surely a spy would know better than that." She couldn't imagine him taking public transportation of any kind, let alone an unauthorized taxi. "What do government program officers drive?"

"Their sister's minivan."

"Kiefer keeps touching me with his foot," Chelsea complained from the backseat.

From that point on their talk was limited to settling minor disputes and answering hundreds of questions.

Garrett chose the back roads rather than the highway. "We're sightseeing," he said when Kiefer, unhappy about having to sit in his car seat, rebelled over the length of the drive.

To distract the children, Isabelle taught them to sing a Dutch lullaby she'd learned in Amsterdam. She didn't speak the language very well, but she loved the sound of the words—Slaap kindje slaap, daar buiten loopt een schaap. Een schaap met witte voetjes, die drinkt zijn melk zo zoetjes. Slaap kindje slaap, daar buiten loopt een schaap.

An hour later, they followed a long, winding road along the coastline to Martinique Beach. When they got to the provincial park area, they drove through protected wetlands before finding a parking spot close to the change rooms. Isabelle held Kiefer's hand as they walked along the boardwalk to the stairs that led through the grassy dunes to the beach.

They dropped their picnic basket, towels, and blankets near the base of the dunes. The children headed straight for the water, the girls shrieking when they got wet above the knees because it was cold, but it didn't stop them from playing in the waves. Kiefer, however, plunged in with a splash. Garrett stayed close to his side to keep him from going into water deeper than the bottom of his shorts. It was too easy for a small child, especially one who loved the water, to be knocked down by the surf and drawn out with the pull of the tide.

Seawater foamed around Isabelle's ankles, numbing her feet. A stiff breeze blew steadily in from offshore, whipping her hair across her face. She hugged her arms across her chest and shivered in the lightweight summer dress she'd donned over her bikini. She hadn't expected the beach to be so cold in July.

"You swim on that side of me, along the edge of the beach where it's shallow," Garrett was saying to Kiefer, pointing to his right, "not on this side, out to where the sharks will eat you." He jabbed a finger to his left, where nothing but whitecaps and a yawning blue ocean touched the horizon.

Isabelle clicked her tongue in disapproval. "I'll let Cheryl know who to blame if he has nightmares tonight."

"This kid doesn't get nightmares. He gives them." Garrett took his eyes off Kiefer's bobbing crown for a few seconds long enough to take note she was shivering. He straightened, pulled off his gray sweatshirt, and tossed it to her. Underneath, he wore a white T-shirt tucked into black board shorts. "Here. Put this on. You can keep it dry for me."

She tugged it over her head, too cold to refuse such a simple, kind gesture. It was warm from his skin, and smelled good, like spice-scented cologne. It was like donning an embrace.

"Why don't you go sit on the blankets, out of the wind?" he suggested.

She hesitated. She was being paid to look after the children and he was supposed to be on vacation. "I don't want to impose on you."

"My nieces and nephew aren't an imposition. I like playing with them. I don't see them often enough."

The children were enjoying themselves. So was Garrett. She was in their way, interfering in family time. She walked up the beach to the blankets, spread one out on the sand, and sat down where she could keep an eye on the children, just in case, and also be alone to think.

She needed to come up with a plan. She watched Garrett, playing in the water with the children. Soon she might have no choice but to trust him. She needed to know more about him first. Who—what—he was. She couldn't come right out and ask. If he was CSIS, he'd only lie to her. She huddled deeper into his sweatshirt, digging her toes into the sun-heated sand.

She'd have to find out who he was on her own.

CHAPTER FIVE

ALTHOUGH SHE HID IT well, Isabelle had been preoccupied all day. She'd been miles away, her attention only dragged back by the children or a direct question from him.

As they dusted sand off little bodies in the parking lot and fastened the kids in their seats, Garrett wondered what might be the cause. If it had been something he'd said or done. While he conceded he'd done plenty—far more than he should have—he didn't think he was the main reason behind her distraction. She'd been unfazed by their kiss. There'd been nothing unusual about her behavior after they finished stretching that morning, either. The only time Isabelle had been alone all day was when she'd gone to her room to get dressed. It was possible she'd made a phone call, or gone online. If she'd gotten a message from her father, or news of some kind, it hadn't been good.

Garrett knew she suspected what he was. Earlier, she'd turned the conversation to spies—but she'd been fishing for information long before that.

Suspicions were one thing. All he had to do was make sure she didn't find out for certain.

He took the highway home from the beach rather than the back roads this time. Kiefer, the chief troublemaker, soon fell asleep in his car seat. The girls chattered with each other, occasionally firing a question into the front for the adults to answer.

After they got home and unloaded the van, he excused himself.

"I have a few emails to respond to," he said, and abandoned Isabelle with the children.

Upstairs, in his suite, he checked to see what her recent online activities had been. She'd read the CSIS Act. How…boring. Bet that put her to sleep. Then he frowned at his computer screen. For a woman who didn't like to shop, she spent a lot of time in online stores. She'd been on one site at 7:36 a.m. She appeared to appreciate handcrafted gold jewelry, the stuff that was one-of-a-kind, yet he couldn't recall her ever wearing a single item of it. He hadn't seen any jewelry when he'd gone through her belongings, either. The belly ring appeared to be all she possessed.

He dug a little deeper into her browser history, but found nothing unusual. She'd clicked a link for one of the cheaper rings, but it was on backorder and she hadn't lingered, or tried finding one similar to purchase, instead.

I'm not much of a shopper.

He flipped the screen closed and drummed his fingertips on the laptop. Maybe she just liked to look, but he didn't think so. If there was a hidden message, however, he wasn't getting it.

He didn't get anything about her.

He heard voices outside and went to the window. Two of Peter's teenage nephews, who lived on the farm, had come over to use the pool to cool off after their work in the fields. Beth, Chelsea, and Kiefer were begging Isabelle to let them swim too, never mind that they'd spent the better part of their day in the ocean already.

Isabelle was laughing at something one of the older boys, Chris, was saying to Beth. The wind caught the skirt of her pretty yellow sundress, lifting it enough to show plenty of tanned thigh, and Garrett watched the boys' gazes shift to her legs, just for a second.

It seemed the pool wasn't the only attraction around here for sweaty, teenage boys.

Isabelle left Chris and his brother Max in charge of their younger cousins while she walked toward the house, no doubt to get towels.

Garrett turned away from the window. While he knew Chris and Max well, and they were really nice guys, they weren't little children. At seventeen, Chris was already taller than Garrett. He should probably go down and make sure she wasn't uncomfortable having them here.

The pain in his leg tweaked as he headed for the door of his suite, reminding him of how her fingers had felt on his skin as she'd worked the muscle. The memory of the way she'd tasted as he'd kissed her, pressed against the wall in this very hallway, came back all on its own. He paused at the head of the stairs. Maybe he had been the cause of her preoccupation today after all, a possibility that raised an unpalatable question: How far was he willing to go to get information from her?

Touching her—kissing her—weren't part of the job. Those were things he'd done on his own, for pleasure, because he'd wanted to. Isabelle, on the other hand, wasn't in the best position to be able to tell him she'd rather he didn't. Her last employers had let her go without pay for this very reason. She had no reason to think that wouldn't happen to her again.

Somewhere below, he heard a door close. She'd likely gotten whatever she'd come for and gone back outside. He changed his mind about joining her at the pool. He hadn't been planning to go outside for her peace of mind, but for his. If she could handle Khao San Road late at night, she could manage the harmless attentions of two teenage boys.

Later on, when they both had a few free minutes, he'd talk to her alone, only this time, he'd come on less strong. He'd make arrangements for them to go running together again, and for giving her driving lessons. He'd ignore all that smooth skin. Those wide eyes. The full lips. He'd work on building a friendship.

He got his chance not long after dinner.

Once the dishes were cleared and the children settled in the family room, tired out from a long day and waiting for bedtime, Isabelle said she had a book she wanted to finish and went upstairs.

Peter lounged on one leather sofa, his socked feet propped on a cushion. He still wore a dress shirt and trousers from work, but he'd ditched the tie and jacket. Garrett sat in a recliner in front of the television, comfortable in his T-shirt and shorts. Cartoons were on, and he was collecting ideas for Christmas presents based on Beth's reactions to the commercials. Chelsea sprawled across Garrett's lap, her thumb in her mouth and a finger twirling a rust-colored curl. Her eyelids kept drooping, then popping open, as she fought to stay awake. Cheryl was in Peter's office at the front of the house, the door open in case someone needed her, working on some papers she'd brought home.

Garrett leaned over the armrest of his chair and prodded Peter's shoulder. "Hey. Your son's asleep on the floor."

"So he is." Peter sat up. "Kiefer, come on, bud. Get up. It's time for bed. Cheryl!" he called to his wife. "Grab a kid."

A half hour later, all three children had brushed their teeth and were in their pajamas. Despite loud protests that they weren't sleepy, Kiefer and Chelsea passed out seconds after their heads hit the pillows. Beth had a book Cheryl was reading to her.

Garrett and Peter met on the second-floor landing outside Kiefer's bedroom.

"I'm going to go watch the news upstairs," Garrett said.

"And I'm going to go book family seats for that one-way space trip to Mars," Peter replied. "Since we're exchanging alibis."

"Funny."

His brother-in-law, normally so easygoing, lowered his voice. He shot a glance loaded with significance at the third floor. "Seriously, Garrett. About Isabelle. You might be able to get away with a lot more than most people when it comes to nosing around in someone's business, but we have privacy laws in this country—harassment ones, too—and I'm an elected official. I've got to be seen following the rules. Try to remember that, okay?"

Which was why Peter should never have interfered in the first place, Garrett longed to point out, but didn't. If Isabelle had gone off to some third party home where her employers were totally ignorant of his investigation, as he'd planned, there'd be no problem for them. Now Peter wouldn't have ignorance to use as a defense. While it might not create problems for him with the public since any official reports would be whitewashed anyway, it well could in private, among the other elected members of Parliament.

"I'll remember," Garrett said.

He climbed the stairs to the third floor. He walked past his door and approached Isabelle's. He listened outside for a few seconds, but heard no sounds within. He rapped on the door with one knuckle, not wanting Peter or Cheryl, only a level below, to hear. He got no response, so he knocked louder.

Still nothing.

She couldn't have fallen asleep. It was barely past eight o'clock. The sun hadn't yet set. He inched the door open. Maybe she'd taken her book to read in the bath.

When he peered into the suite, the bathroom door was open and the room was obviously empty. The bedroom door through the sitting area was also wide open. That room, too, was empty.

"Isabelle?" he called softly, still mindful of Peter and Cheryl.

No answer. The television was off. Her book and laptop both sat closed on the coffee table.

Where could she be?

There was nothing else up here but a linen closet, and an attic that took up the other half of the third floor. Garrett went out in the hall. He rattled the attic door, but it was locked. Cheryl didn't want the children playing in there and accidently trapping themselves in.

That left only one place.

He shook his head, half impressed, one hundred percent intrigued. He'd known she was bold and had shaky ethics. The big question now was whether she was snooping or stealing. In all fairness he'd searched her room first, so he couldn't cast stones. Since all of his files were password protected, if she were snooping there'd be no real harm done. Stealing was a different matter, but he didn't think that was on her agenda.

He opened the door to his suite. She was curled in a ball on the sofa with her hands clasped under her cheek, her breathing even and deep, as if she were sound asleep.

Pink flip-flops, with flowers that fit between the toes instead of thongs, peeked out from beneath the edge of the sofa.

He didn't believe she was sleeping. Not for a second. But, wow, he admired her boldness and ingenuity, although maybe not the insult to his intelligence.

He didn't try to wake her. Instead, he strode over to his laptop bag. She'd searched through it, he could tell at a glance. He always kept the flap in a particular position so he'd know. His laptop was inside, but he didn't bother to check if she'd tried to use it. If so, she'd have wasted her time.

He went to stand beside the sofa. Dark lashes dusted her cheeks. Caramel streaks from the sun mixed into the natural deep brown of her hair. She wore it loose, but right now it was twisted away from her face in a knot to expose the slender length of her neck. With the skirt of her thin dress smoothed over her buttocks and tucked between her thighs for modesty, she looked like a barelegged angel. So young and innocent. If anyone saw her right now, they'd never believe for a second she could survive the back streets of Southeast Asia on her own, simply by using her brains.

Friendship, be damned. He wanted her. It amazed him how much. Desire, hot and liquid, swirled in the lower regions of his abdomen. It rushed through his veins. He wrestled it back.

One thing at a time.

"Did you find whatever you were looking for?" he asked.

She rolled to her back and opened her eyes. She stretched her arms over her head. Her skirt hitched a few more inches up her legs, but that part of her act might be accidental.

"Are you CSIS?" she asked in return.

If she'd hoped to catch him off guard with her question, she'd be disappointed. She was hardly the first person to try. "Why would you think I'm CSIS?"

She stared up at him. Her gaze was very direct as she recited her list. "The ugly tourist clothes you were wearing when I met you in Bangkok that are so not your style. You see every little thing happening around you. You got me out of a country currently under military rule on very short notice, no questions asked. You had an RCMP friend meet me in Ottawa and take my passport. I conveniently end up at your sister's. Now you show up for a month's vacation, when your sister tells me you rarely take one for more than a few days, and usually during the Christmas holidays." She presented her final item with a faint air of triumph, the pièce de résistance. "You aren't annoyed to find me in here."

"Are those the only reasons you've got?"

"You need more?"

He didn't ask if her suspicions about him had more to do with her father's activities than his clothes and connections. If he wasn't admitting to anything, he couldn't expect honesty from her. He perched on the cushions beside her, his hip against hers, resting his hand on the back of the sofa so she couldn't escape.

He leaned forward so that his lips hovered a few inches above hers. "I'm a government program officer. One who kissed you, just this morning. I went running with you, which I hate. I let you coerce me into yoga, which I hate even more. I believe I've made my interest in you very clear. So why would I be annoyed to find you in my room tonight?"

Amusement, not caution or fear, backlit her eyes and spread to her lips. She tried to push him away. "That's one more reason I think you're not what you say you are—your excessive interest in me. I'm hardly your type."

She had no idea exactly how much she interested him, and in how many different ways. He settled his weight on her so that her hands were trapped between their two bodies. "Tell me what my type is, then."

"Someone more like your sister, an independent woman with a high-powered job of her own. One who wouldn't need you, but rather, want you. And you wouldn't frighten her."

Those were no more than guesses on her part. Good ones, but based on assumptions and not actual observation. His mouth twitched. "Don't forget she'd have to be beautiful."

She slid her gaze away from his, then back. "That, too."

"Independence could be better defined as intelligence." He shrugged. "I like clever conversation. And maybe I like to be needed as well as wanted." He debated telling her how beautiful he found her, but decided to leave that to actions, not words, and leaned another inch closer so that their lips almost touched. He could feel the slight hitch in the rise and fall of her breasts as she sucked in a sharp breath. His groin stirred again, with more insistence this time. "I'd also like to point out that I don't frighten you. Not nearly as much as I should. Now. What were you looking for?"

"My passport."

She was lying and he didn't care. He wanted her to trust him. He had no intention of trusting her in return.

"I don't have it." Not in this room.

Her eyes sparkled with a more rueful kind of humor. "So I discovered."

She looked so tempting, with the smile in her eyes and the flush to her cheeks... The part of him that housed his soul said he was an asshole for thinking up ways he might get her to betray her own father. How far was he willing to go to get what he wanted?

How far was she?

He dragged one palm up the length of her arm to her naked shoulder, then trailed his fingertips along her throat, savoring the satin texture of her skin, taking his time, careful to gauge her reaction. To see if she liked what he did. His thumb caught the leap of pulse at the base of her jaw. His own jumped in response. He slid his fingers into the thickness of her hair at the nape of her neck, then pressed his mouth hard against hers. His tongue stroked the plumpness of her bottom lip, teasing it open, so that he could taste her better.

A soft moan escaped her. She freed her hands to tug at the hem of his T-shirt. Seconds later, she smoothed urgent palms over his abdomen, her fingers clutching at his hips, clinging to him. Heat burst inside him. He cradled her closer, letting her feel his hard, rigid length between them. He dragged his mouth from hers to kiss the line of her jaw, then the side of her throat, the dip of her collarbone. She still wore her bikini. He untied the strings of the top at the back of her neck. The silk of her dress blocked his passage to the swell of her breast. With the tip of his finger, he edged the fabric aside.

A debate warred inside him. He needed to get close to her to get to her father. But this wasn't work. It felt far too personal. Somehow, he had to keep the two things separate.

She was breathing faster now, short little sighs of encouragement, accompanied by a restless writhing of her slender body beneath his that had his groin throbbing with a rising need and sent any second thoughts scurrying from his head.

"Êtes-vous le SCRS?" she asked again, this time in French, a puff of sound scuttling along his heated skin. Are you CSIS?

There was an underlying note of uncertainty in her question that drew him up short. The fact that she'd asked him in French reminded him of the preoccupation she'd tried so hard to hide all day. That something was troubling her.

Trust went two ways. He couldn't do this. Not when they weren't being honest with each other. Not when it might lead to her not liking herself very much later.

And hating him.

He straightened the front of her dress, sparing a moment of regret for the shiny belly ring he'd hoped to have his tongue on by now. He re-tied the strings of her bikini top, slowly, with an even greater reluctance. He'd found his limit, but he wasn't as confident she'd found hers. "I'm a government program officer."

He was also an asshole. He'd made light of her ethics, when his own were equally questionable. He was the one in the position of power right now. She hadn't come in here for this. He could feel it.

She stayed where she was, looking up at him from the sofa's cushions with an inscrutable expression, whatever she was thinking a mystery. Only the slight unsteadiness to the rise and fall of her breasts indicated she wasn't as calm as she pretended.

"What does a program officer do?" she asked.

"Besides keep reckless women out of trouble?" He brushed a thumb across her bottom lip, unable to resist the temptation. Her self-control fascinated him. "Why do you ask?"

The obvious battle warring inside her spilled onto her face. He waited, curious to see what she'd decide. If she'd admit what she'd really come to search his room for.

Then, "My father is missing," she said. "You must have connections. I'd hoped you might be able to help me find out what might have happened to him."

CHAPTER SIX

HE HADN'T DENIED BEING CSIS. Neither had he confirmed it. But she'd had too many weeks of worrying over her father to care any longer.

Besides, she'd found nothing among Garrett's belongings to indicate he was anything other than what he claimed. Maybe, if she told him as little as possible, and made it sound as if she were the overprotective daughter of an irresponsible man—in other words, the truth—he might be persuaded to do her this one additional favor on top of everything else.

She hadn't intended to persuade him in this way, however. Hot embarrassment burned the backs of her eyes. She had no words for what had just happened between them. No good explanation. She blinked away her emotions. Thank God he'd shown some common sense and hadn't gotten as carried away as she had.

Garrett continued to sit on the sofa beside her, his hip pressed to hers, one hand braced on her thigh. His thumb played with the skirt of her dress, bunching the fabric. "You told me you aren't as close as you once were. What makes you think he's missing?"

"I've never gone this long without hearing anything

from him before." She couldn't admit that she had gotten a message—of sorts. It had almost been worse than none at all. She kept her eyes on his, afraid he might see too much. "My father sometimes loses track of time, and doesn't understand why I worry about him when he's out of touch."

"When was the last time you heard from him?"

"Christmas. We spent the holidays together in Amsterdam. I think he has a girlfriend in the city, but he's never introduced us."

"Why do you think he has a girlfriend?"

Because it was preferable to her actual suspicions.

"The usual reasons," she said. "Late night phone calls he didn't want me to overhear. Him slipping out for a few hours at a time without telling me, and bringing me back little presents as an excuse. He never wanted to go far from the hotel when usually he likes to attend concerts and parties, and visit with friends." Love for him pinched her heart as she tried to explain his behavior. Yes, he was irresponsible. But he adored her. She didn't doubt that. "We spend New Year's Eve in the Netherlands whenever we can because he enjoys the celebrations. He's like a little boy during the holidays." She felt her smile fade. "I thought a girlfriend might be the reason I haven't heard from him in so long."

"Where were you both headed after New Year's?"

"I was on my way to London to meet up with the family I was working for, then to Thailand. He was staying in Amsterdam for a few more weeks. After that, I don't know. He was supposed to meet me in Bangkok." She made a face. "You know what happened next."

Garrett was frowning, as if dissecting everything she'd said. "Did he seem worried to you? Afraid?"

"Not at all." And he hadn't. If anything, he'd seemed

too eager. Excited about something. She hadn't seen him so happy in years. That was why she'd really hoped he had a girlfriend. She wanted him to be happy—but for the right reasons.

"Where were you staying in Amsterdam? Do you have an address?"

She gave him the name of the hotel.

"You said he likes to visit with friends. Have you tried to contact any of them to see if they might know where he is?"

She shook her head. "I only know their first names."

"You travel to the Netherlands for New Year's whenever you can, so your father can party with friends, and you don't know their names?" The casual movement of his thumb stopped. "So here's the thing, Isabelle. I don't believe you really thought he had a girlfriend. I also don't believe you haven't heard from him. In fact, I don't believe much of what you've told me. And if I don't trust what you're telling me, I can't—won't—help you."

Panic swelled inside her. He had to.

"I have nowhere else to turn," she said.

"Then you have no choice but to be honest with me." He tugged on her skirt for emphasis. "Sometime between our run and breakfast this morning, you must have gotten a message. Tell me what it was, and how it was delivered to you, and then, I'll see what I can do."

She couldn't tell him. If she did, it would only add an extra layer to her story that went far beyond that of a flighty, irresponsible father. She didn't know what kind of trouble her father was in and she wanted him found, not jailed. While CSIS didn't make the actual arrests, they handed any intelligence they gathered over to the proper authorities. The end result was the same.

"Never mind. I shouldn't have bothered you."

She tried to wriggle past him off the sofa, but he caught her around the waist with one arm and drew her back to sit beside him.

"I understand you're worried," he said, "and you want to protect him, but have you ever stopped to consider that whatever he's doing, or involved in, might hurt other people?"

The implications of his words—the bald statement of her own fears—left her gasping inside. He already knew—or had strong suspicions—that her father was involved in questionable activities, but he had no more proof of it than she did. "My father would never hurt anyone."

"So you have considered the possibility, then."

Yes, but she refused to believe it. What worried her far more right now was that he was the one who might get hurt. Or he already was.

The seconds ticked away in the silence of the room. Garrett waited, apparently unbothered by it. She suspected he could sit here all night. The air conditioning kicked in, the sudden hum startling. She stared at her fingers, lacing and unlacing them in her lap. She was the one who'd asked for his help. At the very least, she'd have to tell him about the message.

"He had a few friends he didn't want knowing too much about me, or his movements. Acquaintances, rather," she amended. "Friends of friends. So when I first went to boarding school, he came up with a secondary way of communicating with me that only the two of us would understand. That way, no one would know where or when we planned to meet."

Garrett sighed. "And you didn't think any of this was…I don't know…strange?"

"Of course I did. But we've always lived private lives.

He wanted to keep his work separate from me as much as he could." She'd also known not to ask questions she didn't want answered. "He's not a bad person. I told you he works for a security management company. It's highly confidential."

"And convenient." He rubbed his forehead. "Tell me about the message. I want to know how you got it."

"Promise me you won't tell anyone."

They were sitting very close together. His thigh pressed tight against hers. She could feel the bunching of his muscles with every slight movement. The alert tension in him. "Would you believe me if I made such a promise?"

She lifted her chin and met his eyes. "As a program officer, yes."

Humor hooked the corners of his mouth. "Then as a program officer, I promise."

Which meant his promise was worth nothing. She'd give him the message, but not the delivery system. "He sent me an email from an IP address routed through Portugal. He said I'd be unable to contact him, and will have to wait for his next message. I'm tired of waiting. It's already been months."

The hint of a smile in his eyes faded. Caution spiked. This wasn't the man who'd kissed her. Touched her. The one who'd complained about running and made fun of yoga, and took his nieces and nephew to play at the beach. Staring hard at her now was the intimidating man who'd grabbed her wrist on Khao San Road.

"You're lying to me about the IP address."

She couldn't breathe. "How do you know I am?"

"A good guess."

Outrage kicked in, hot and defensive, as she figured it out. He was monitoring her email. He really was CSIS.

Even though she'd been certain of it already, the confirmation blindsided her. Suspecting and knowing were two very different things.

Her chest ached from holding her breath. She stood, forcing herself to expel air. Anger wasn't going to get her anywhere. Whatever CSIS was investigating, her father was nothing more than a starting point for them. They were after bigger fish, like the people her father was hiding from. Having CSIS find him first could only be positive. "I—"

A knock came at the door, disrupting her thoughts. A new panic surfaced. This was Bangkok all over. She didn't want to be caught in her employer's brother's private suite. If she were dismissed before she'd saved any money, she'd be back where she started.

Garrett must have had similar reservations about them being discovered together. He jerked his head toward the bedroom. She hurried across the thick beige carpet on bare feet and into the other room, easing the door closed behind her with a silent snick of the latch, then pressed her ear to the white, wooden panel.

Garrett opened the door. Peter stood in the hall.

"Cheryl wanted to know if you'd like to watch a movie with us," he said.

"Love to," Garrett replied. "Give me ten minutes. I have something I need to finish, first."

"Great. I'll go see if Isabelle would like to join us." Peter made a move toward her door.

"I'll ask her," Garrett said.

Peter stopped. He gave him a look that Garrett knew

well. Too well. "What difference does it make who asks?"

"She doesn't like to interfere with your family time. She's more inclined to say yes to me."

"Your logic makes no sense whatsoever. I think I'll take my chances." Peter knocked on her door. He waited a few seconds, then knocked again. "Isabelle?" His hand dropped to his side as he turned back to Garrett. He shrugged. "Guess she's either asleep or busy. If you want to check with her one more time before you come down, go ahead. We'd hate for her to think she isn't welcome. She spends too much time alone as it is."

"I'll do that," Garrett said.

Peter paused in the open doorway. "This weekend, the whole family is hosting a neighborhood barbecue at the farm. You and Isabelle are invited too, and—" His words broke off as he stared at something on the floor behind Garrett.

Mentally, Garrett ran through the contents of the room after he'd come in and found Isabelle on the sofa pretending to be asleep, trying to recall anything that might catch Peter's interest. He saw his laptop—and a pale pink pair of flowery flip-flops, lying partially hidden under the edge of the sofa. He also pictured the closed bedroom door.

The two men looked at each other. Neither spoke, each waiting for the other to go first. Peter finally broke the standoff. Concern filtered into his expression.

"Maybe I should add one more warning to what I gave you before," he said, very quietly.

Garrett kept his response equally soft. For both his family's sake and Isabelle's, and the forward momentum of his investigation, it might be best if he let Peter think this was exactly what it looked like—which it well could have been.

"I'd like to point out that we're in my room, not hers. She's a grown woman. I didn't lure her in here."

"Fair enough," Peter said. "But she's had a hard go of it the last few months. Using her to get information would be beneath you. Keep that in mind." He spoke louder. "The movie starts in ten minutes. Don't forget to ask Isabelle to join us."

"I won't."

Garrett closed the door. He rested his palm on the frame and closed his eyes, trying to think. His brother-in-law's disapproval, although it bore weight, was the least of his worries. On the investigation front, things had gotten a great deal more complicated.

Marc Beausejour had found a simple system for moving around the internet undetected and his daughter knew what it was. It had to be in one of the sites she'd been visiting this morning. An unexpected disappointment lodged in the pit of his stomach. Deep down he'd wanted to believe in her, but so much of what she'd told him spoke of complicity, either direct or indirect.

He heard her come out of the bedroom.

"Did he know I was in here?" she asked when he turned to face her.

He tried to decide how much, if anything, she'd overheard. "He wants us to watch a movie with them."

"I thought I'd go to bed early."

His lips twitched.

"Alone," she added, cutting him off, although she couldn't quite smother a small smile in response.

That hint of a smile had him pursuing the invitation with more aggressiveness. "Watch the movie instead. You'd be doing me a favor. I don't want to feel like the third person on someone else's date night."

"What movie is it?"

"Does it matter?"

"Of course it does. Some movies are more 'date night' than others."

"If this one turns out to be too 'date night' you and I can play cards in the kitchen," he said.

"Or you could simply excuse yourself and go to bed. You don't need me there for that," she pointed out.

He was determined to win. "If you expect a favor from me, then you can at least do this one thing in return."

Wary hope sprang into her eyes. "You'll see what you can find out about my father?"

"I will if you tell me how he contacts you. I need something to start with."

How much he told her of what he uncovered, however, depended on her level of cooperation. He watched the conflict play out across her face as he waited for her to make up her mind. When she did, she spoke in a rush, the words tripping over each other as if she were afraid to hold them back in case they stopped coming.

"Through an internet shopping site. He sets up an account for selling handcrafted gold jewelry. I always look for a particular ring. If it's available, I send him a personal message through the buy link. If it's on backorder, it means I'm not to leave a message or try and contact him. He'll come to me when he can. This morning, the ring was on backorder."

"And you've already been waiting longer than normal."

She ran a hand up and down one of her arms. "Something's wrong. I know it."

Garrett could think of several things about this that were wrong, especially when he considered what information Beausejour might be exchanging using similar setups. Worse, at least to Garrett, was that while

Beausejour hid from the problems he created, he left his daughter to fend for herself on the streets of Bangkok, or wherever else he'd abandoned her over the years, exposing her to a great deal of danger. The people searching for him would have a much easier time finding her. He had to know that.

The man was a bottom feeder.

Between what she'd just told Garrett, and what he'd gotten from her internet usage, he had enough information to turn over to the computer people at headquarters so they could begin to pin down Beausejour's location. With a little luck, it wouldn't be much longer before they had him. Then they could find the supply chain for those weapons systems parts.

He also had to factor in how much involvement Isabelle really had in all of it. Right now, CSIS's only interest in her was in finding her father. Garrett prayed it stayed that way, because he'd have no choice but to turn her in, too, if he found out otherwise.

"Stop worrying. I'll do what I can," he said.

Stark relief flooded her eyes. She slid her arms around his waist and hugged him, pressing her cheek into his shoulder. "Thank you," she said. "He's very dramatic. He likes playing games of intrigue. But he's not a bad person."

He turned his head to bury his face in her hair. It smelled of fresh ocean air, citrus shampoo, and sunshine. Her impulsive gesture, and the erratic beat of her heart against his ribs, told him more than words how much her father meant to her, and of the enormous stress she'd been under. Peter was right. The last few months had been hard on her. Far more than she'd let on. The next ones would be too, because while she might not want to believe the worst of him, Beausejour was involved in criminal activity. None of this would end well.

Their ten minutes were up. He disentangled himself, stooped to reach under the sofa, and handed her flip-flops to her.

"Let's go watch that movie," he said. "You might have to wake me up in the morning if you want me to go running, though. Five thirty is too early for me."

She held her hair away from her face with one hand and slid the pink flower of each sandal between her toes with the other. She glanced up at him, more carefree than he'd yet seen her. "If you aren't ready when I am, I'm going running without you."

"I'll be ready."

Guilt pinched his conscience. He'd wanted her trust. Now it seemed he had it.

No. This wouldn't end well at all.

He was ready and waiting for her the next morning, and the morning after that.

But, other than running together, he kept his distance and spent his days with either the children or Peter. Since it was difficult to look at him without remembering how it felt to have his hands on her, or the touch of his mouth against hers, which unsettled her, Isabelle avoided him, too.

By Saturday afternoon he still had no information for her, and while Isabelle had known it would take time, she was growing increasingly anxious. What concerned her most was how much of what he uncovered, if anything, he'd be able to share.

She wasn't certain how much of it she wanted to know.

Where her father was, and that he was safe, would be enough. When he did contact her, however, she planned to speak to him about her future. She was done living like this, in both uncertainty and fear. The fact that CSIS was now interested in his activities should serve as a wake-up call to him that it was time to change careers.

She peered in her bathroom mirror and applied makeup with a light hand. The entire Mansford clan was holding a barbecue at the farm this afternoon, something they did every year, and Cheryl had insisted she come. Weekends were hers to do with as she pleased, but without a driver's license, she had nowhere else to go, so she'd agreed. Besides, there'd be plenty of people and it would be nice to meet more of the neighbors.

A driver's license.

Her hand stilled in the process of outlining her lips with a nude blush. She'd forgotten about it when she'd discovered it would take her six months to get beyond the learner's permit stage. There'd seemed little point. But to get a learner's permit she'd need identification, and a Canadian passport would fulfill all the requirements.

The strapless muslin sundress she'd chosen to wear had a lavender-colored, form-fitting bodice over a tight waist with a white-and-lavender flowered design. The short, flared lavender skirt broke mid-thigh, swirling around her legs when she moved. It was an impulse purchase she loved but had never worn. She didn't examine too deeply the reason she'd chosen to wear it today, or to put on makeup. Sometimes it was simply nice to feel pretty.

When she finished her makeup, she secured her long hair in a loose knot at the nape of her neck with a hairband. A quick glance at her watch, and the pitter pat of three pairs of little feet in the hallway outside her suite, told her it was time to go.

Small fists pounded on her door and the one next to it. "Izzy! Uncle Garrett! Mommy and Daddy are ready!"

They stepped into the hall at the same time, coming face to face with each other. Their gaze met over the children's heads. Isabelle saw what she thought might be appreciation in his.

He let out a low whistle. "That," he said, "is a nice dress."

Pleasure bloomed inside her. He looked good, too. He'd changed into a short-sleeved white cotton shirt and navy cargo shorts, and his light brown hair was still wet and spiky from a shower. She caught the familiar scent of spice cologne. Before she could thank him for the compliment, or pay one of her own, he shifted his attention to the children.

"Go where?" he asked. "I heard they canceled the barbecue because of rain."

Chelsea frowned up at him. Her curly red ponytail bounced as she gave a vigorous, negative shake of her head. "It's not raining."

"He knows it's not," Beth said, with her seven-year-old superiority. "He's trying to trick you."

Kiefer tugged on Isabelle's hand, dragging her toward the stairs. "I want to go."

The weather was too hot for the children to walk, and it would be dark before they came home, so everyone piled into the minivan for the short drive.

The main farmhouse, where Peter's oldest brother lived, sat a half mile up a steep hill in the opposite direction Isabelle always took for her run. Along with the house, the property had two barns and a large machine shed. Beyond the farm, the pavement ended and became a dirt road. Another brother lived across from the farm, while the Mansfords' parents owned a smaller house a mile farther along the dirt section. Isabelle hadn't met them yet. She'd heard the elder Mr. Mansford was confined to a wheelchair.

The large front yard was full of vehicles, everything from half-ton trucks and SUVs to sports cars. Peter parked the van alongside a farm truck. Garrett opened the sliding back door and lifted the girls out while Isabelle freed Kiefer from his car seat. Garrett set the little boy on his feet, reached for Isabelle's hand to steady her as she stepped to the ground, then closed the door behind her. Peter and Cheryl took charge of the children, leaving Garrett and Isabelle to walk together as they skirted the side of the house and followed the noise to the back yard.

The enormous stone patio and flower gardens had been strung with lights and circled with bales of hay for seating. To the far left, outdoor games had been set up. To the right was a canopied bar, complete with bartender, tables, and chairs. Three enormous barbecues belched smoke near the steps to the house and the open kitchen door.

Isabelle slowed when she saw the size of the crowd. Garrett placed a hand on the small of her back, urging her forward so that she stayed by his side.

"There's nothing to be shy about," he said into her ear.

"I'm not shy."

Far from it. But she preferred making a quiet entrance so she could study people first, which was impossible when she was with Peter and Cheryl, who knew everyone.

It turned out Garrett knew quite a few of them, too. She'd been introduced to a dizzying amount of relatives and neighbors before he finally abandoned her near a thick hedge of dark pink roses with two of Peter's cousins,

Mary and Thea, middle-aged sisters who liked to travel. They were planning a fall trip to Paris and wanted her advice.

"We went to New Zealand last year, but for the most part, we're cross-border shoppers and stick to the US," Mary said. "This will be our first trip to Europe. We don't speak any French so we're a little worried about finding our way around."

"Just a little, though," Thea added. "Not enough to stay home."

Their enthusiasm sparked a flare of wistfulness. Isabelle had traveled her whole life, and still, she never tired of discovering new places, or revisiting the ones that she'd loved.

"You won't need French," she assured them. "The metro is very economical, and easy to use for getting around the city. Don't buy anything from anyone who approaches you on the streets or outside of the tourist attractions, don't give money to children or anyone with a sad story who claims to be hungry, and you'll be fine."

Someone pressed a plastic glass of red wine into her hand. Garrett was back. He'd heard the last bit of her advice.

One eyebrow shot up. "Don't give money to anyone who claims to be hungry, hmm? What if they're desperate?"

When he'd asked her for an explanation as to why she was trying to sell her passport she'd told him she was hungry. Any desire to make light of the situation died. Her desperation and worry remained far too fresh. She didn't ever want to go through that again.

Bangkok seemed so far away now.

"Feeding them would be a kind gesture on your part," she conceded. "One greatly appreciated. However, giving money to strangers requires a very big leap of faith." She couldn't resist a small reminder that he wasn't as altruistic as he presented himself. "Unless, of course, you expect to get something in return."

Garrett took a sip of his beer and held her gaze. "How mercenary. Sometimes simply taking that leap is its own reward."

There'd been no leap of faith on his part. He hadn't given her money. He'd bought her a plane ticket. They both knew he hadn't done it out of the goodness of his heart, either. He'd taken her passport away.

She was grateful to him nonetheless. He'd fed her before he knew anything about her. Whatever his real reasons for helping her were, and regardless of his true level of altruism, he'd been kind to her.

Thea spoke up. "Since my subtext is even worse than my French, let me see if I understand you both correctly—we shouldn't give money to strangers unless we believe in a higher Being, but taking them out to dinner is okay," she said. "Got it. What if they want us to go dancing with them after our meal?"

Garrett rubbed the back of his neck. "Then you should keep a close watch on your passport. I hear those things are better than gold on the black market."

"They're certainly difficult to recover if they're taken from you," Isabelle added. "Embassy staff isn't as helpful about finding lost items as one might expect."

"We're plenty helpful," Garrett said. "It all depends on what's missing, and how it was lost."

Mary nudged her sister. "My subtext is better than yours. We should check to see if Catherine needs any help in the kitchen." She spoke to Isabelle. "It was lovely to meet you. We'll have to talk again later. But watch out for Garrett. This boy is trouble."

They thought he was flirting with her. In a way, she supposed he was. He simply wasn't after what they assumed—at least, not with any serious intentions.

The two women left, leaving them alone by the hedge. A honeybee landed in the yellow center of one of the unfurled rose blossoms, its wings quivering as it worked.

He took another long sip of his beer. "You heard the woman. Watch out. I'm trouble."

"I'm not sure you should be flattered." Isabelle clutched her plastic wine glass. "She didn't say what kind of trouble. And she called you a boy. I feel as if I've been handed the responsibility for your good behavior."

He peered at her over the top of the bottle, his hazel eyes unreadable. "If I misbehave you can spank me."

Isabelle laughed. She couldn't help it. It was the deadpan delivery. Plus, the thought of anyone spanking Garrett for any reason was ludicrous. No one would dare.

"I'm sensing you aren't into BDSM."

That only made her laugh harder. "And you are?"

"I've never tried it." His eyes dropped from her face to the low line of her bodice, then back. "But probably not," he admitted. "I prefer a more gentle approach."

Her laughter died. They weren't alone. At least a hundred people milled around the large yard. Yet here, partially hidden behind the high rose bushes, when he looked at her that way, she felt as if the entire world had suddenly emptied. She remembered in great detail how it felt to be kissed by him.

To have the light touch of his fingers slide against her bare skin.

"Let's go for a walk," he said.

It wasn't a good idea. She didn't want anyone to think

she had any romantic thoughts toward Cheryl's brother. She didn't. She was tired of intrigue. She had even less interest in spies. To Garrett, no matter how decent he might be, she was a piece in a game involving her father and he enjoyed playing it more than she liked.

She was going to follow him anyway, without hesitation, because if he'd been flirting before, something warned her he wasn't now. Despite the heat of the day, a chill chased up her spine.

They set their empty drinks on the ground. Garrett took her by the elbow and guided her around the end of the hedge to the other side. Fields of grass and foot-high corn stretched to the base of the hill a half mile distant. From there, a dense green blanket of forest began, spread out for miles. A narrow strip of pavement cut a ribbon-like trail through the trees.

He led her along a narrow gravel footpath that hugged the side of the house, then disappeared into a dense stand of poplars and maple trees a hundred yards beyond. The sounds from the barbecue soon faded, replaced by the rustle of leaves and the sigh of the wind. A squirrel chattered from the branches above them.

He stopped in a small clearing. By now, dread had built all sorts of worst-case scenarios in her head. Her father was dead. He'd been kidnapped by terrorists. A plane he'd been on had gone missing over the Indian Ocean.

What he said was unexpected. "We can't get a fix on your father's location through the site you gave us. He logged in using a VPN—a virtual private network. We can trace it back as far as the RBN and can't get any farther."

Isabelle was lost. "What does any of that mean? What's an RBN?"

"The Russian Business Network. It's an internet service provider with connections to the Russian mafia." A muscle in his jaw worked. "It means your father is serious about not being found."

CHAPTER SEVEN

IT MEANT SO MUCH more than that. Whether or not her father was involved with the Russian mafia, the fact that a Canadian citizen was hiding his tracks behind the RBN, a well-known internet service provider for cybercrime, wasn't a good sign.

Garrett had received the call from the CSIS director in Ottawa telling him that Beausejour couldn't be tracked a few minutes before the munchkins came banging on his door. Oh, and by the way, the director had added, those missing weapons parts turned up in Pakistan. He'd wanted to have Isabelle formally detained on suspicion of facilitating terrorism because she'd been in Thailand when someone brokered the exchange. He believed there was a possibility she'd been acting on her father's behalf.

That was when Garrett had started to sweat. CSIS had a very broad mandate. Deliberately so. It gave the director a great deal of latitude in making judgment calls.

"Terrorism is a stretch in this case, don't you think? Canada doesn't have any issues with Pakistan," he pointed out.

"They've never signed the Nuclear Non-Proliferation Treaty. Therefore, the illegal sale of weapons systems with nuclear capabilities, even parts, to any Pakistani aircraft maintenance company can be viewed as a potential act of terrorism."

"She's a Canadian citizen. She has rights. She's hardly a terrorist."

The director sounded tired and stressed out, and increasingly impatient. "I'm less concerned about her rights than I am in saving innocent lives, and possibly avoiding a war. If there's even a remote possibility she can implicate even one of the people involved, then I'm willing to have her formally detained. She's got to know something useful about Beausejour. I want him found. You have three weeks left. If she hasn't helped you pin him down by then, I'm stepping in. In the meantime, whatever you do, don't lose her."

So here Garrett stood. Her father had a large number of strikes against him, making him a potentially bigger player than CSIS first thought, and he'd stepped away from the plate, leaving Isabelle to pinch hit for him.

At least her confusion was real. Garrett thanked God for that. He had no idea why her father had gone into hiding, or who he was hiding from. Until Garrett had caught Isabelle trying to sell her passport, Beausejour had been of no more than a passing interest to CSIS, and since no one but the CSIS director knew of Isabelle's connection to Garrett's investigation, there was no way Beausejour could have learned they'd gotten more curious.

But if he wasn't hiding from CSIS, then who?

That VPN activity leading to the Russian Business Network made Garrett nervous. She'd said herself that her father had tried to keep his work separate from her, but if Garrett had made the connection, someone else could, too.

"I thought you were going to tell me he was dead," she said.

She was shaking, he realized with a jolt. Remorse punched him in the gut. He hadn't been particularly sensitive. To him, Marc Beausejour was a criminal involved in espionage. A traitor to his country. But to Isabelle, he was someone she loved very much.

He couldn't simply stand here and watch her try to hold herself together, pretending he wasn't affected by her distress. He wasn't trying to break her.

His shoes crunched in the thick layer of dead leaves, broken twigs, and pine needles on the path as he took two steps across the small distance between them to draw her to him. He pressed her face against the front of his shirt, stroking her hair. With the heel of his other hand, he rubbed the small of her back. She balled her fingers into fists and rested them beneath his rib cage. To his enormous relief, she didn't cry.

"How much trouble is he in?" she asked, speaking into his chest.

"I'm not sure. It could be a lot."

Dappled sunlight sprinkled the clearing. The tangy scent of spruce and mulched earth settled into his lungs. She was quiet for a long time.

"I really don't know anything," she finally said. "I never wanted to know."

Her not wanting to know was what worried him most. She had to have recognized that her father's activities weren't legal, even if she couldn't say for sure what they were. While Garrett didn't give a damn what happened to her father, what happened to her was a far different story. She was in trouble, too. Her cooperation now would go a long way toward minimizing the extent of the damage. Those New Year's parties in Amsterdam had to be a big part of all this. So far as he could tell, they were the only thing consistent about Beausejour's movements in recent years, and she'd lost contact with him not long after the last one. Unfortunately, this was July. Garrett couldn't wait another five and a half months and continue to keep Isabelle off the CSIS radar. He had three weeks.

He continued rubbing her back, allowing his thoughts to wander for a few seconds. He still hadn't quite figured out what it was about her that attracted him so much. Yes, she was prettier than he'd first thought. And in the dress she was wearing, even prettier still. But it was more than that. He liked the feel of her against him. He liked touching her. He liked making her smile.

He counted to ten and shifted his focus back to his investigation. Right now, he needed names. Even first names would be something. He put several inches of space between them, shifting his hands to her elbows so he could maintain physical contact with her, but also study her face.

"Why did you tell me your father's name is Leon?" he asked.

"Because it is. Marc Leon. But only very close friends call him Leon," she admitted. "My mother did."

The name might have no significance. Or, it might have a lot. "At these parties in Amsterdam, what did people call him?"

He watched her mull over the question, a tiny frown clouding her eyes as if she were trying to remember—or decide how much was safe to reveal. She'd be excellent at poker.

Then, "Most people call him Marc."

"Most? Not all?"

Another prolonged silence. "I'm so used to hearing him called by both names I don't really notice anymore."

Yet when he'd asked for her father's name in Bangkok,

she'd been quick to give him one he might not recognize rather than the one most people knew him by. "How many people can you think of who always call him Leon?"

"Three, maybe four. He was Leon at my boarding schools, too, so that was how any correspondence he received from them was addressed."

They'd have needed a mailing address. There might be old records on file he could use to track Beausejour's movements while she'd been at school. He could cross-reference them against anything she could remember of where her father had been during those years, and what CSIS already knew. At least it was a place to start.

"I'll need to know the schools you attended," he said. "I'd also like the names of anyone you can think of at that last New Year's party. Even if all you can remember are their first ones."

Isabelle shrugged off his hands, no longer meeting his eyes. She smoothed her hair, refastening the knot at the nape of her neck. "There's no need. I've heard enough to satisfy me that there's no use in my trying to find him. He'll turn up when he's ready."

"You asked for my help," he reminded her.

"And you gave it to me. Thank you. I'll just have to be more patient and wait for him to contact me again."

"It's not quite that simple."

"It is for me. You have to understand my father. Life is a game to him. When I was a girl in boarding school, he'd arrange secret meetings for us. I'd sneak out of my dorm after hours and we'd go to the theater together, or to the bars, or sometimes, just for a run late at night. On holidays, he'd send me a train ticket to a large city, like Paris, where he'd meet me. From there, we'd head to another destination. Belgium, perhaps. Italy. It was never by the same route, and it was always an adventure. I can see why his travel habits might trigger alarms. But he's more like a spoiled teenager than some..." She struggled to find the right description. "...Third world warlord." She tipped her head back and looked at the sky through the filter of trees. "We both know you're CSIS." When he tried to speak, to remind her he was a government program officer—also the truth—she cut him off. "My father works in international security management. Sometimes maybe he protects people he shouldn't. I don't want him going to jail for being guilty by association."

She was scared. She didn't like what she was hearing. She had to be starting to understand that her father's desire to keep his movements secret had always been less about protecting her than himself.

Nobody ever thanked the messenger.

"This might go a bit beyond association," Garrett said carefully. CSIS had been thorough. They shared information with worldwide organizations. Nothing in Beausejour's history indicated he worked in international security, legitimate or otherwise. That was a story he'd told her and she chose to believe it.

"You're wrong."

He caught her wrist. She continued to refuse to look at him. He had to be careful not to push her too hard, but to play on her fears. "If we find him, we could be saving his life."

She wasn't listening to him anymore. "We should head back. Cheryl might need my help with the children."

"It's your day off," he said. "She and Peter can look after their own kids."

"Everyone will think we've gone off to be alone together."

"We have." Garrett looked around the empty clearing. "We are."

He understood what she meant. While he might not mind what anyone thought, it was plain that she did. She'd found herself in a similar position before and it had cost her a job. Still, he couldn't let her go back to the barbecue looking as if her world had ended. She was still shaking. Reality had begun to set in. Peter would take one look at her, and this time, Garrett was the one who'd be tossed out on the street.

So yeah, maybe he minded, too.

"Come here." He tugged on her wrist, still loosely clasped in his fingers, then settled his hands on her bare shoulders, loving the feel of all that smooth, sun-kissed skin. He ran his fingers down the length of one arm, then moved his hand to the sleek swell of her buttocks, tucking a knee between her thighs to draw her against him.

Instead of pulling away, she pressed closer, and the way she was looking at him, her emotions so carefully guarded, yet with a tiny spark of hope in the depths of her eyes, pricked his conscience. He couldn't begin to imagine what her life must be like. She had no home. No one to depend on. In another six weeks, when the kids went back to school, she'd be jobless again. He'd have to speak to Peter about finding her something with a real future to it that would give her independence from her father and his criminal associations. If she wouldn't look out for herself, he'd have to do it for her.

He was falling for her. He could admit that much, at least to himself.

Then don't break her.

He cupped her face between his palms and kissed her, lightly, because he couldn't stop himself. "Everything's going to be okay, Isabelle."

"Je l'espère, vous avez raison. Je l'aime mon papa. Il est un homme bon," she murmured under her breath.

I hope you're right. I love my father. He's a good man.

Her father wasn't a good man. Garrett knew it. He didn't think she really did. But he couldn't say for certain, which raised a question—how much of this attraction he felt between them was real on her part, or about her using him to protect her father?

She was so very different from any woman he'd ever met. He couldn't figure her out. But in the end, even though he might understand her using him for her father's sake, he'd never be able to get past it. And if she decided he was only using her to find her father, she might never forgive him, either.

They had good reason not to trust each other.

He brushed his thumb against the silky skin of her cheek, contemplated kissing her again, then instead, let her go. He shouldn't be taking these chances. Not when it came to his emotions—or hers. Some matters would have to wait until others were resolved. Right now, she'd choose her father over him.

"You're right," he said. "We should get back."

When they reached the edge of the trees, Isabelle stopped. She tipped her face toward him. Any doubt or indecision she might have harbored was long gone. Again, he was reminded of the general fearlessness of her. One had to dig deep to find the vulnerability. He'd managed to reach it, but it remained buried.

"I'll tell you everything I can remember about names and places," she said. "In return, all I ask is that you keep an open mind about my father."

Garrett's words about possibly saving her father's life had

resonated, reflecting fears she hadn't wanted to acknowledge.

Beneath the fragile shell of calm she'd cocooned herself in, panic simmered. He could well be working a security job somewhere that had somehow gone wrong. If so, she should be doing everything she could to make sure he was safe. Since CSIS would be far more interested in her father's connections than him personally, she didn't know why she'd even hesitated to agree to give Garrett the information he wanted.

Yes, she did. Because he unsettled her with his soft kisses and gentle touches, even though it was nothing more than deliberate misdirection on his part. It made her not trust him. Twice now, when she hadn't shied away from him, he'd stopped.

At least she knew he had a line he wouldn't cross. Or, maybe he didn't find her attractive at all, and was simply a very good actor—but only up to a point. Whichever it was, it was important that she stand her ground with him. He'd exploit any weaknesses.

"Fair enough," he was saying, his expression steady and serious. "But what if it turns out I'm right?"

It didn't bear thinking about. "Then I'm the one who'll have to be open-minded."

"Let's hope you're the one who's right, then," he said with a trace of wry humor. "Because we can't have that happening."

His kindness toward her was almost unbearable. She and her father must seem like such train wrecks to him. A knot hitched in her heart. The worst of it was, right now it was true.

They walked out of the trees to find what seemed like fifty children running and screaming around the side of the farmhouse, at least ten of whom sported enormous water guns. Bringing up the rear were Chris and Max, Peter's oldest nephews.

One of the younger children, a redheaded boy of nine or ten, swiveled to return fire at Max with the water gun he carried. As he turned, he caught the toe of his shoe on an untidy pile of firewood.

Isabelle watched the disaster unfold in slow motion. The water gun went flying in one direction, the boy in the other. As he fell to his hands and knees, he cracked his head on a stick of wood. Immediately, blood erupted. Seconds later, so did tears.

Max, a lanky fifteen-year-old, reached him first. By the time Isabelle and Garrett got there, the teenager already had him on his feet. Blood streamed from a cut above the boy's temple to drip off his chin.

"What's your name, bud?" Max was asking him. "Is it Fred? Ralph?"

The boy made a fierce face at Max through the blood and tears. "It's Ronan."

Max looked up at Isabelle and Garrett with relief. "That's the extent of my first aid knowledge," he said to them.

Around the cut, Isabelle could see that the boy's forehead had started to discolor and swell. The swelling slowed the bleeding, but so far showed no signs of stopping it.

"Will you let me have a closer look?" she asked Ronan.

Garrett made a gesture for her to move aside. "Here. Let me take care of this. You're going to get blood all over your dress."

"No!" the boy cried, shrinking away from him. "I want Isabelle to look at it."

"And I want to see it," she assured him. "The lump is

very impressive." She knelt down and put her arm around his shoulders, not at all concerned for a dress she rarely wore and wouldn't miss. A wardrobe was disposable. She replaced it as needed, to suit whatever climate and situation she found herself in.

Max peeled off his T-shirt and handed it to her. "It's clean. You can use it to stop the bleeding. I'll go find Anna."

Anna, a friend of Cheryl's, was Ronan's mother. She was also a nurse, Isabelle recalled. She sometimes dropped off Ronan and his sister to play in the pool with the Mansford children.

Very gently, not wanting to cause more distress, Isabelle pressed the T-shirt to Ronan's forehead. He was steady on his feet, and his pupils looked normal, which came as a relief. Head wounds tended to bleed a lot and sometimes looked worse than they were. When she peeked under the T-shirt, however, she could see that the cut was deep and gaped open at the edges. He was going to need stitches.

"Well, monsieur Ronan," she said, "let us go in the house while we wait for Max to find your mother." She took him by the hand, carefully holding the T-shirt to his head with her other one. "If we put a big enough bandage on it and cover your eye, we can make you look like a pirate. You are very lucky," she added. "Not every boy your age can say he was wounded in a shootout."

Ronan's tears stopped. He ran his free wrist under his nose. "Do you think it will leave a scar?"

She squeezed his fingers. He looked a great deal happier at that possibility than his mother was likely to be. "Most assuredly."

The other children hovered nearby, concern and uncertainty on their young faces. Now that the worst of the drama was over, Chris, who had been quietly watching out for them, took charge.

"There are new kittens in the barn," he said. "Who wants to see?"

While the children took off across the yard to the barn, weaving through the jumbled maze of parked cars, Isabelle led Ronan to the rear entrance of the house. Garrett trailed behind them. Inside there was a large mudroom, with a laundry tub next to the washer and dryer, and an adjacent shower and toilet enclosure. Two pairs of stained coveralls hung on hooks beside the bi-fold door to the toilet. Isabelle boosted the boy onto the counter beside the laundry tub. Clean towels sat on a shelf above their heads.

A few minutes later Ronan's mother Anna, a pretty woman with curly red hair that matched her son's, arrived to take over. After a quick look, she confirmed that a trip to the emergency department for stitches was in order.

"I don't want stitches. I want a scar," Ronan said.

"Don't worry, you'll have an awesome one," his mother replied, ruffling his hair with her fingers. "And it depends on the doctor, but they'll probably tape your cut closed rather than stitch it. In fact, I'm going to tape it right now to see if I can stop the bleeding."

Isabelle found a first aid kit under the counter and set it beside Anna, then handed towels, antiseptic, and bandages to her as required. In no time, Anna had Ronan's cut cleaned and bandaged, and mopped the rest of him off as best she could with old towels.

"You're the best patient I've had all day," she said to her son when she finished, giving him a hug. "You're very brave." She turned to Isabelle. "Thank you so much. I—Look at your dress!" she exclaimed in dismay. "I'm so sorry. Let me have that cleaned for you. If the stains won't come out I'll replace it."

Isabelle looked down. She had large splotches of blood on the front of her bodice and skirt, as well as the tops of her sandaled feet. Her hands and arms, too, were coated in it. The strong, coppery odor bit her tongue. She reached for a bar of soap so she could wash it off her skin in the laundry tub. "There's no need. I hardly ever wear it and it cost very little."

Anna left with Ronan. Isabelle rinsed the last of the soapy water down the drain and nudged off the faucet with her elbow.

"I'll take you home so you can change," Garrett said from behind her.

She spun around. He'd been so quiet she'd almost forgotten he was in the room. Now, with his unwavering attention focused on her, he seemed to fill every corner. He gave the impression of a man who could fix anything.

And yet he'd had no problem stepping back and allowing her to take control of a minor crisis. She hadn't expected that from him.

Neither did she expect him to take one of the dampened towels, get down on one knee, and begin to scrub the blood off her legs and feet with it, holding the back of her thigh with one hand as he worked on each leg with the other. She rested her hands on his broad shoulders, balancing her weight, gazing down on his bent head. She couldn't shake the memory of how good it felt to be held against all that solid muscle.

"You're very good with blood. Sports injuries, too," he said, addressing her toes. "You'd make a great nurse."

"A nurse? Why not a doctor?"

She'd meant to tease him about sounding sexist, but he

wasn't playing along. He looked up at her in perfect seriousness. "Would you want to be a doctor?"

She'd never considered it before now. Absently, she smoothed her palms along his shoulders. She'd been well educated. She could get into a good post-secondary school if she applied herself. But without her father, she had no money for it. And did she want to spend all those years studying?

"No," she confessed after giving it some thought. She had no burning desire to be a nurse, either. "I like children. I like looking after them. If you love them, they love you back. You get to bring out the best in them and encourage their talents to grow. You're shaping the future of the whole world. There's nothing I'd rather do."

When compared to his sister and her friends, and their accomplishments, she sounded like such an underachiever, but she didn't care. She did like children. They were the same everywhere. Innocent. Genuine.

He straightened, tossing the towel in the nearby washing machine with the others they'd dirtied. Bright rays of sunshine streamed through the window, splashing warmth across the slate floor. "Then that's what you should do."

She heard the frown in his voice, and the unspoken implication. There must be jobs with greater security than being an au pair. She already knew that. Someday, she'd need to do something about it. A lifestyle of poverty had worn thin very fast back in Bangkok. Once she'd settled things with her father, she could consider other options.

"You think I could be more," she began, driven by pride to defend herself, "but—"

He interrupted her before she could finish her explanation. "I don't think you could possibly be more than you are right now."

The quiet words, spoken with such sincerity, flooded her with unexpected pleasure.

"Thank you." She could think of nothing else to add, too afraid of sounding as if she'd read more into them than he meant.

He made a move toward her. "Isabelle, I—"

The exterior mudroom door slammed open. They both jumped. A little girl skittered into the room and made a beeline for the toilet enclosure.

Isabelle reached for a bottle of laundry detergent on one of the shelves with a shaky hand. "I should put Max's T-shirt in the washer to soak with the towels."

"I'll get the keys to the van from Cheryl so I can take you home to change."

He vanished.

She started the washer and added detergent. When she was finished, she went outside to wait for him. She could hear the children playing in the barn. The smell of cooking pork from the barbecue floated on the air.

It wasn't long before he came loping across the yard, keys jingling in his hand.

He didn't speak during the short drive. When they got to the house, he turned off the engine. It ticked in the sudden quiet. He rested one arm on the steering wheel and faced her, then reached over and touched her hand.

"Whatever happens with your father, you don't have to face it alone. I'm here for you."

They both knew that wasn't true. He wasn't here for her. He was here to find out what she knew, which was very little. She withdrew her hand, easing it from beneath his and settling it in her lap. She laced her fingers together.

"Why do you do this?" she asked.

"Do what?"

"Follow me around. Look at me as if you find me fascinating. Touch me, and say nice things to me. And then, you pull away as if you did nothing at all." She gave him a self-deprecating smile. "I've already agreed to tell you everything I know. There's no need for these games."

He didn't deny it, as she'd expected him to. He didn't look sorry for it, either. He raked fingers through his sun-streaked hair, spiking it in the front. He looked like an older version of Kiefer, but much sexier.

And far more dangerous to her peace of mind.

"I do it because I can't help it," he confessed. His eyes glittered. "You seem to bring out the worst in me."

She could say the same about what he did to her. She'd never had a problem with insecurity, or of second-guessing herself, before he came along. All she could do was continue to pretend that he didn't affect her. That her heart didn't race when he looked at her that way.

"Do your worst, then," she said. "One of these days I'm going to call you on it."

His voice dropped, developing a seductive edge to it that sent a frisson of awareness through her body. "You don't want to do that."

She clenched her fingers more tightly together. "No?"

"Absolutely not." He reached for the door, popping it open. "You might discover I'm not bluffing."

"Wait a moment."

He paused, half turning, one foot already on the ground. Amusement—and something more—lit his eyes as they met hers. "You're calling me on it already?"

Despite the tension twisting her insides, she couldn't help but smile. "Not quite yet. You said you'd give me driving lessons."

His gaze lingered on her face. "I did, didn't I."

She pried her fingers apart to appear more relaxed. "In

order to apply for my learner's permit, I need identification that meets the Access Nova Scotia requirements. That would be my passport."

"I see your problem." He tapped his fingers on the steering wheel as if puzzling out what to do. "I'm sure something can be arranged." He slid the rest of the way out of the driver's seat and stood in the driveway. "Come on. We should hurry." He leaned in, one arm resting on the hood of the van, to repeat her words from earlier. "Everyone might think we've gone off to be alone together."

CHAPTER EIGHT

HE GAVE HER FULL credit. She'd called him on one of his bluffs. He hadn't seen it coming, either.

Giving back her passport was no real issue. It had been locked in Peter's desk the whole time. Withholding it had become more of a game to him than anything. She couldn't use it without being flagged in the system. He'd know her every move.

No, he'd kept it because he liked to torment her. He was going to miss the anticipation of finding her searching his rooms for it again. She really did bring out the worst in him.

He returned the passport to her on Sunday night, after dinner. Monday morning, after Isabelle called to confirm the hours of operation, they loaded the children in the minivan and headed to the city, where she'd write her test for her learner's permit. After that, they were to meet Cheryl for lunch at a restaurant near her law office on the waterfront.

The Access Nova Scotia office was buried in a large industrial park on the outskirts of the city. Garrett took the children for ice cream while they waited for Isabelle. When they returned she still hadn't come outside to the parking lot, so Garrett rolled down the windows and shut off the engine. Heat rose in shimmering waves off the pavement, but a good cross breeze blew through the van so it wasn't unbearable. He settled in, prepared for the inescapable complaints of "I'm bored." Isabelle had braided both girls' hair and they looked pretty cute, but it wouldn't be long until Kiefer, who was sitting between them, got his hands on one and had a sister crying. He checked his watch.

He'd give it five minutes.

In the meantime, he mulled over the latest information from his director. They'd spoken the night before. Garrett had given him the address of those parties in Amsterdam as well as the first names of several guests.

"It's a private penthouse," the director had said. "Belonging to a Canadian ex-pat by the name of Bernard Vanderloord. Ring any bells?"

"No," Garrett confessed. "Should it?"

The director's voice was grim, and loaded with inference. "He's a close personal friend of our Minister of Defence. They went to school together."

Things had become far more interesting. And troublesome. CSIS reported directly to two ministers—Defence and Justice—but at the discretion of the CSIS director. While this had wide-ranging implications, overall, it could only be good news for Isabelle. "I take it we won't be filing any official report?"

"Not at this point."

Which meant her name would be kept out of the investigation, at least for the time being. If they managed to find her father, CSIS would have no further interest in her. Not if her involvement was as peripheral as she claimed.

Garrett wasn't as confident about that as he'd like to

be. If she'd been at a party with guests who had connections to high-ranking government officials, she had to know. These people wouldn't be low profile. Not by anyone's definition. And Isabelle was very astute.

"So what would Marc Beausejour be doing at a party in Amsterdam thrown by the Minister of Defence's close personal friend?" he wondered out loud.

"That's what I'd like to know." Garrett heard a rustling of papers. "As far as we can tell, Vanderloord is clean. If the Americans or the Brits know anything to the contrary, they haven't shared it. But he has some serious international business connections in aerospace and defense. Unfortunately, the names Beausejour's daughter gave you don't match any of them. These parties Vanderloord is throwing must be private. It's possible they're nothing significant, just a gathering of friends. The best way to find out for sure is to question Beausejour."

It was also the safest. Beausejour remained the lowest hanging fruit on this particular tree. "Should I ask Isabelle if she recognizes Vanderloord's name? Show her a photo?"

"No. We already know who he is and that Beausejour is involved with him somehow. Let's not give away anything more than we have to."

The conversation had left Garrett on edge. He'd lain awake half the night, listening for Isabelle's quiet movements in the adjoining room, going over all their conversations in his head to see if he'd somehow been played. If he had, he finally concluded, it was for her father's benefit. He'd already known she'd do anything for him. What he couldn't determine was how much her father was willing to do to protect her. He'd bet even Isabelle didn't have an answer for that.

"Do you have a girlfriend, Uncle Garrett?" Beth asked

from the backseat, bringing his thoughts back to matters at hand.

He glanced into the rearview mirror. "All kinds of them. Why?"

"Izzy could be one of them, couldn't she?"

The conversation was about to get interesting. "Who says she'd want to be?"

Beth blinked. "Of course she would. Ronan's mom thinks you're hot. She says if Izzy doesn't grab you, she will."

It was his turn to blink. "I'm pretty sure Ronan's mom was joking. Ronan's dad might not be onboard with that."

"Why not? If you have lots of girlfriends, why can't Ronan's mom have boyfriends?" Chelsea asked.

This was turning into one of those discussions that might make Cheryl mad. Last time, he'd ended up practicing yoga. "I'm not married to any of my girlfriends. Ronan's mom is married to his dad. It makes a difference."

"Why?"

"Are Mommy and Daddy married?" Kiefer interrupted.

"Of course they are, stupid. How do you think they got us?" Chelsea's green eyes met Garrett's in the mirror. "Is that why it's different? So you can have babies?"

Tailing arms dealers in Thailand had been less stressful than this. He rubbed the back of his neck and shot a desperate glance around the parking lot, searching for some sort of distraction. A crumpled piece of pink paper tumbled across the pavement, coming to rest beneath a nearby Lexus. Other than that, nothing moved.

What was taking Isabelle so long?

Right on cue, as if she'd been waiting for his mental distress flares to go off, she emerged from the building. But she wasn't alone.

Garrett craned his neck, trying to get a look at the tall guy who was holding the door and talking to her, his head bent over hers. He was young, maybe a year or so older than Isabelle, and sported a suit and tie. Off the rack, Garrett noted. Decent quality. He carried a frayed laptop backpack with earbuds dangling by wires from one of the pouches. Some kind of computer tech, if he were to guess.

She laughed at something he said. Garrett tried not to stare at them. She had that whole fresh-faced cheerleader look going on, with the long ponytail, cropped, tight T-shirt, and skimpy, hip-grazing shorts. All that bare, toned leg...

It wasn't that her outfit was inappropriate. She was dressed no differently than any other young woman her age. He also knew exactly what she had in her closet, and other than the oversize T-shirt and shorts she'd been wearing in Thailand, and a few lightweight dresses, she didn't have much to choose from.

But Garrett didn't like the way the other man was looking at her. She looked far too pretty when she was smiling the way she was now.

"Never mind, Uncle Garrett," Beth said, her blonde head leaning out of the window. She had a streak of strawberry ice cream under her chin. "Isabelle's already found a boyfriend."

"She can have more than one," Garrett said. "She isn't married."

"This one's as hot as you are," Chelsea added.

"Do you even know what that means?" he asked her. He didn't plan to take the blame for this if she did.

She crinkled her freckled nose. "It means cute, right?"

"Close enough. Maybe you should say that instead of hot."

"Don't you think he's cute, Uncle Garrett?"

"I'm not supposed to think he's cute." His attention

was on the guy's body language, not his level of hotness. Cuteness. Whatever.

Isabelle's companion handed her a piece of paper. She read it, smiled again, and appeared to be thanking him as she stuffed it in her shorts pocket. Garrett wasn't close enough to hear, but that was his best guess as to her side of the conversation. Then she looked around and saw the minivan. He sank down in his seat and turned to the kids in the back, not wanting her to think he'd been paying any attention.

He could hear her footsteps approaching. Her sandals made soft slapping sounds against the sticky asphalt. She opened the passenger door and hopped in, waving a plastic card in triumph.

"One hundred percent," she said to the kids. "What do you think of that?"

The girls, however, remained focused on their previous, unfinished conversation.

"How many boyfriends do you have?" Chelsea asked her.

Isabelle, used to children, wasn't fazed by the apparent randomness of the inquiry. "Seven," she said without hesitation. "What about you?"

"I only have two."

"Does your father know about them?" Garrett asked Chelsea. He turned to Isabelle. "Who's your new friend? Is he number seven or eight?"

Her face blanked for a second. "You mean the man I was just talking to?"

"That would be the one. Do you always collect phone numbers from strangers?"

"Of course not. I spoke to him for two minutes. He gave me a website address for an online running room he thought I might find helpful."

Garrett didn't need to ask how the guy knew she was a runner. One look at her legs said it all. He didn't believe for a second that running was what he'd been interested in when he'd looked at them, either.

"Really? Want to check that piece of paper he gave you more closely?"

She pulled it from her pocket and read it. "Hmm. I guess he really is number eight," she said to Chelsea.

Garrett shook his head. "You can't possibly be so naïve as to think running was what he had on his mind."

She held up the strip of paper for him to see. On it was the link to a running website.

"You think I don't know when a man is interested in me?" she asked. She paused for a beat. "Or that I can't tell when he's playing games?"

Garrett might play games, but they were serious. She had to know he was interested in her. "No," he said. "I don't think you can."

"He was hot, Izzy," Beth spoke up.

Isabelle's head whipped around, her eyes widening. "Excuse me?"

Garrett bit back a grin. "She means cute. According to Ronan's mother, I'm the one who's hot."

"I wouldn't read too much into that. The last time she saw you, she had a lot on her mind."

"Don't you think Uncle Garrett's hot, Izzy?" Chelsea asked.

Isabelle looked him over. Her grave expression became one of pity, as if she hated to be the bearer of bad news. "He's cute enough, I suppose."

He'd love to know what she really thought. He was fairly confident she considered him better than cute.

Chelsea played with one of her braids, a frown of deep concentration on her face as if she couldn't quite figure something out. "If you have seven boyfriends, how will you know which one to marry?"

Garrett sighed. "You just aren't going to let this go, are you?"

Isabelle nudged his knee with hers as she rested her arm along the back of her seat to speak past the headrest. "If I have seven boyfriends it means I'm not going to marry any of them. It means I like them and they're nice, but I don't think any of them are special enough to marry. If one of them was that special to me, he would be my only boyfriend."

"Nice answer," Garrett congratulated her.

Kiefer weighed in with his opinion. "You could marry Uncle Garrett. He's special."

Four pairs of eyes, including Garrett's, turned on Isabelle. He lifted his eyebrows in a silent challenge. C'mon. Let's hear you talk your way around this one.

She ignored him. "Of course he is. And he deserves someone special, too. But finding two special someones who are right for each other can take months, even years. It's a big decision. You don't want to get it wrong."

"I disagree. If it takes months or years to decide," Garrett said, "then they're probably wrong for each other right from the start."

"I'll marry Isabelle," Kiefer said, as if the matter were settled. "I think she's special. She thinks I'm special, too. Don't you?" he demanded of her.

"I certainly do," she replied. "If you still want to marry me when you're old enough, then I'm all yours."

Kiefer had lost interest by now, more intent on ending the conversation than pursuing it. He grabbed one of Chelsea's red braids in his fist and gave it a hard jerk. "When are we going to see Mommy?"

Garrett rolled up the windows so the whole industrial

park didn't have to hear Chelsea's screams, letting
Isabelle deal with the problem because she was better at
soothing hysterics, and eyed his watch. Ten minutes. The
boy was growing up.

Once Isabelle had the backseat under a cease and
desist, he drove the minivan out of the park and onto the
highway, headed for downtown and the harbor front. She
was good with children, no doubt about that. She wasn't
the kind of woman who couldn't make up her mind about
things, either. She knew what she wanted—and she
wanted to work with children.

She also liked traveling, and remained unflustered in
high-pressure situations. Garrett shifted gears and moved
into the passing lane. She'd make a good relief worker.
An excellent one, in fact. She spoke several languages and
understood third world living conditions.

But he'd been in disaster zones. While she might be
good at it, and he didn't doubt she could take care of
herself as much as anyone in those types of situations, he
didn't like the idea of her working in one.

Isabelle wasn't his responsibility, however. It didn't
matter what ideas he liked. She'd agreed to help him find
her father. She'd said nothing about letting him take
charge of her life.

They had lunch with Cheryl at one of the many taverns in
Historic Properties, a tourist area along the city's
waterfront. They ate outside, on the patio. The street was
narrow and very steep. The historic sandstone buildings
were juxtaposed with newer, more modern glass and steel.
At the foot of the hill, the white-capped waters of the

harbor sparkled in the sunlight. If Isabelle turned, she could look up to the Citadel, an old fortress dating back to 1749, which crowded the skyline.

Isabelle barely tasted her order of fish and chips. Her entire body felt numb. The scrap of paper burned a hole in her pocket. Someone had tapped the Mansfords' landline on her father's behalf. When she'd made a call that morning to check on the times for writing her test, they'd found out where and when she'd be. Good fortune had found her alone long enough for a messenger to slip her a note.

So yes, Garrett, I do know when a man is interested in me.

All of her father's precautions, ones she'd taken for granted—or chosen to disregard—were now cast in a new light. The Mansfords' landline—belonging to Peter, a Member of Parliament, and Cheryl, who worked for a prominent law firm—had been tapped. Peter received personal calls at home from constituents with problems. One of the last cases Cheryl had worked involved a high-profile homicide. To tap their landline went far beyond a harmless safety precaution. What if Peter or Cheryl got in trouble over information someone stole from them?

Her father couldn't possibly do something like this and be in international security management, as he'd claimed. Whatever he was involved in, Garret was right. It had to be bad. Nausea churned in her stomach as another realization struck her. She'd given CSIS information on her own father, the man who loved and raised her.

She could feel Garrett's eyes on her.

"You okay?" he asked.

"The sun's in my eyes." She squinted, making Kiefer giggle.

"Would you like to trade seats with me?" Garrett was wearing sunglasses and she wasn't.

"Thank you, but no. Then I wouldn't have such a great view. From here I can see everything."

After lunch they walked Cheryl back to her office, then headed to the boardwalk that skirted the harbor. Garrett had parked at an outdoor lot not far from the Maritime Museum of the Atlantic. They spent two hours inside the museum. Behind it was a small playground the children wanted to visit. After another hour, everyone was tired and ready to go home.

"Can we stop at a pharmacy?" Isabelle asked Garrett once they were out of the parking lot. "I'll only be a few minutes. I need to pick up a few personal things."

That was all it took to keep him from asking questions. Men were ridiculous when it came to feminine products.

He pulled up to a fire hydrant on the street out in front. "If I'm not here when you get back, just wait for me. It means I had to circle the block."

Inside the store, she grabbed a box of tampons before heading for the display of disposable phones. She chose the cheapest she could find and purchased the minimum amount of minutes. She also picked up a bag of candy for the children to help disguise what she had in the bag.

When she finished, the minivan was still in the same spot on the street.

"That didn't take long," Garrett said. If he knew she was hiding something from him, he gave no indication.

"It didn't require a lot of decision making," she replied.

When they got home, she ran her purchases straight up to her suite. She stashed the phone under her mattress. It wasn't an ideal hiding place, but neither was it out in plain sight.

Then she sat on the side of the bed and dropped her face in her hands. She could think of no way to tell Garrett about the phone being tapped that wouldn't incriminate her father. Even now, she couldn't begin to comprehend what he must be involved in to be able to arrange such a thing.

She'd tell Garrett tonight, in private, after everyone else went to bed. She'd ask for his help with a problem. She'd admit he'd been right about her father. There was always the possibility he'd withhold where he got the information from, and why the phone had been tapped. Yes, tapping the phone was illegal. But CSIS dealt in information. They didn't always act on everything they learned.

They'd be terrible spies if they did.

Later that night, when the house was silent, Isabelle stood outside Garret's door, gathering her courage. Earlier, he'd been lifting weights with Peter in the basement gym. She hadn't noticed him come upstairs, but she'd heard his shower running, then stop. She'd waited a few minutes, giving him time to dress, but not enough to fall asleep if he'd gone straight to bed.

She didn't know what she'd say to him. How she'd start. Maybe—you were right?

She knocked on the door, a soft rap in case he had gone to bed and wasn't interested in being disturbed. A small thrill of excitement chased up her spine, leaving her hands shaking.

You might discover I'm not bluffing, he'd said to her.

The door swung open. A small lamp beside the sofa

was the only source of light in the room. He'd been reading. He stood a few feet from her, wearing a pair of drawstring pajama bottoms riding low on his hips and nothing else. She'd seen him in less. This was different. His sun-bleached brown hair had been towel-dried but not combed, and was still damp. A shadowy sprinkling of chest hair over a layer of muscle had her fingers itching to touch him.

Warm hazel eyes caressed her. She'd grabbed the same shapeless T-shirt and shorts she'd had on when she first met him. Clean and comfortable, they gave her a sense of protection, which was why she owned them. They were nondescript and didn't draw male attention—the feminine version of a suit of armor. Yet, when he ran his eyes over her, she felt naked.

His smile, slow and lazy, lit his face, making him appear much younger and less...overwhelming. But still dangerous. More so, in fact.

"This is unexpected," he said. His gaze narrowed. "What's wrong?"

She couldn't do this. She couldn't betray her father. Not more than she already had.

"Nothing." She took a step back, wishing she hadn't come. She couldn't expect Garrett to keep such a thing to himself. Not when it involved his sister and her family. He couldn't help her. "Never mind."

"I think I do mind." He caught her hand and drew her into the room, shutting the door behind her with a decisive click. He leaned against it. "If you won't tell me, I'll have to guess." His eyes darkened with humor. "You're calling my bluff."

Her lips curled into a reluctant half smile. He was trying to put her at ease and it was working. "You wish."

"Yes," he said. "I do." His voice deepened and went

smoky, sending shivers through her. "But first, tell me what's wrong."

"I think you might be right about my father." Her answer came out on a soft exhale. The admission hurt her.

"I see." He didn't ask about her sudden change of opinion. He moved closer, placing a hand on the small of her waist as if urging her to dance. His fingers tightened in a quick squeeze of reassurance. "I also told you things will be okay. It will all work out. I'll be right about that, too."

"You can't be right about everything."

"Of course I can."

He sounded so smug and confident. She had the sudden urge to unsettle him. She pressed her forehead to his chest, resting her hands on his hips above the drawstring of his pajamas, and felt the corresponding increase in the beat of his heart as her reward.

"For instance," he said, keeping his tone conversational, "I know that if I were to kiss you right now, this time, you'd stay the night."

It was true. There were so many reasons she shouldn't be here. Yet she wanted him to kiss her anyway. She turned her face upward. As she did, their bodies connected. He bent his head. She rose on the tips of her toes and parted her lips in invitation.

He hesitated, a question in his eyes. Are you certain this is what you want?

Of course she wasn't. That was what made it all the more exciting.

"I call," she said. "Do your worst."

CHAPTER NINE

HE KISSED HER, DEEP and hard and with a thoroughness that left her head in a mixed-up state of confusion.

She forgot why she'd come to him. Why she should leave, although that moment had passed. She lifted her hands to the back of his head, wanting more. She heard a quiet sound—a small sigh of air—and realized it came from her.

He lifted his head. "I warned you," he said, his voice raw. "Last chance."

He wasn't bluffing. She could feel the hard evidence against her abdomen. She shivered, already anticipating what was to come, knowing she could no more walk away than she could stop breathing. She slid her hands down the broad length of his back, pressing tighter against him. "You're talking too much."

His hands went to the hem of her shirt. She caught her breath as he peeled it, slowly, over her head, his knuckles brushing against her skin, his thumbs stroking the sensitive undersides of her arms. The T-shirt landed on the floor. He kicked it aside. His fingers found the clasp on the back of her bra. As he undid it, he kissed the curve of her neck. A sharp, delicious knife of heat lanced through her abdomen. The lacy wisp of fabric followed her T-shirt. Her nipples, peaked and hard, rubbed against the crisp hairs of his chest. The exquisite sensation was torture.

His hands were on her hips now, holding her as he kissed first one breast, then the other. His head dipped lower, his mouth blazing a trail of fire in its wake. He swirled his tongue around the piercing at her belly button. Isabelle's knees weakened, and she had to prop her hands on his shoulders to steady herself. His thumbs hooked into the waist of her shorts, dragging them over her hips and down the length of her legs. She stepped out of them, and was left wearing nothing but a brief pair of panties. He ran a palm up the inside of her thigh, but stopped a breath shy of the thin fabric. His thumb wisped across the warmth of her opening. She gasped, arching her spine.

"You don't talk enough," he said. "I want to hear you ask me for this. No," he corrected himself. "I want to hear you beg."

"Nous allons voir qui est la mendicité," she whispered back. We'll see who is begging.

"We will soon enough." He stood, and in a quick motion, swept her into his arms. She crooked an elbow around his neck.

"You should have more care with your back," she said.

The corners of his mouth kicked up. "My back isn't the part of me I'm most concerned about right now."

The door to his bedroom was open. In a few strides, he'd carried her into the room and deposited her on the bed. He paused to look at her. She could see his face in the pale light of the moon through the open curtains, but couldn't begin to guess what he was thinking. It had to be strange to him to be so physically attracted to someone it was impossible to trust. Already, he might be regretting this.

He reached down with one fingertip and skimmed a line from the base of her throat to the tip of one breast, then to her navel. He toyed with the ring at her belly.

"You always surprise me," he said softly, "with how very beautiful you are."

His thoughts hadn't gone at all where she'd feared. Her insides glowed with pleasure, as much at the sincerity of the compliment as from the heat in his eyes. "You almost have me begging. But not quite."

He hooked her panties in his thumbs and tugged them down her legs. He tossed them aside. His pajamas followed them. Then he was on the bed, kneeling over her, naked and as beautiful to her as he claimed she was to him. He leaned forward and kissed her lips, then her jaw. He traced his tongue over the rim of her ear, nuzzling the sensitive spot beneath it with the rasp of his chin.

She smoothed her palms upward over his ribs, brushing her thumbs along his sternum. His body felt much the same as his personality. Solid. If only things were different between them. That this was real and not a moment she was stealing from him because she was selfish.

He took both her hands in one of his, extending her arms over her head. He kissed her throat, beside her ear. From there, he focused his attention on her breasts. He swirled the pad of his thumb around the nipple of one. He drew the tight bud of the other into his mouth, and gave a light tug with his teeth. As he did, his hand slid between her thighs. He stroked a light finger along the dampness of her cleft, then again, gently exploring at first, before probing deeper. She gasped. A jolt of desire had her arching her hips forward in a silent demand.

This was torture.

His movements stilled. "Tell me what you want from me."

She couldn't begin to describe what she wanted. She had no right to ask for it.

"I want more," she said.

His eyes gleamed in the faint light. "More...what?"

Everything.

She wanted his hands on her. She wanted him inside her. "More of you."

"Then don't move."

He rose from the bed, naked and gorgeous. Isabelle heard him go into the bathroom. Seconds later, he returned to the bedroom, a small packet in his hand. He opened it and extracted a condom.

She extended her hand. "Let me have it."

He held it out of her reach. "Are you begging?"

She considered it. "No. You can do it yourself." She dragged a finger down the length of her torso, from between her breasts to the juncture of her thighs. Hungrily, his gaze followed the movement. "But trust me. It won't be as enjoyable for you."

He tossed the condom in his palm, moving closer to the edge of the bed. "If I give it to you, are you willing to call it a draw?"

"No."

She got to her knees, and settling her hands on the solid curves of his buttocks, dragged him closer. She kissed the hard, flat plane of his stomach, then, trailing kisses lower, she flicked her tongue across the tip of his erection. He sucked in a ragged breath. She cupped him with one hand, drawing the head of him into her mouth, running the tip of her tongue around his rim.

He knotted his hands in her hair, uttering a groan. "Oh, my God."

She looked up at him, a smile on her lips. She ran her

tongue from the base of his shaft to its tip. His entire body shuddered.

"Are you begging?" she asked.

"You're trying to kill me. Yes," he bit out through gritted teeth. He tumbled her onto her back, pinning her down with his weight. He nudged her thighs apart with his knee as he fumbled with the condom in good-humored frustration. "But this isn't over. It's my turn."

He placed the tip of his sheathed erection at her cleft. Instead of thrusting inside her, however, he rubbed it the length of her slickened folds, over and over, until she had to clench her fists to keep from crying out. He entered her deliberately, an inch at a time. Her internal muscles tightened in impatient expectancy. Before she could draw in the full length of him, however, he withdrew. He did it again, even more slowly this time.

Isabelle dug her fingers into the tense muscles bunching at his shoulders, desperate for all of him. "More. Harder. Don't stop."

"Are you begging?" His voice came out sounding strained.

She was beyond caring who won a silly game. "Yes."

That was all the encouragement he seemed to need. He plunged his full length deep inside her, again and again, establishing a rhythm that left her breathless and on the brink of release. She arched against him, meeting his thrusts. Spears of pure pleasure shot to her core. She clutched his shoulders and cried out his name as her orgasm shook through her. He stiffened, and with a muffled groan, he came, too.

She trailed her fingertips along the bumps of his spine. A line had been crossed. Tears blurred her eyes. She wished she could think of something to say that would articulate the enormity of what had just happened, at least for her.

She didn't dare say anything.

She'd held back. Kept something of herself from him. Why would she do that when she'd allowed things to go as far as they had?

Moonlight flooded the bedroom. She sprawled on his chest, her crown beneath his cheek, her breath warm in the crook of his neck. The blankets had been kicked back so that the sheets tangled around their legs. One of her knees pressed against his inner thigh, hugging his leg between hers. Her toe tickled his calf. He ran a finger up and down the line of her hip, enjoying the silkiness of her skin and the slight tremors that shivered through her whenever he caressed the sensitive spot near the small of her back.

"When I was a little girl," she said, breaking the silence, "my mother and I lived in a small town in Quebec with my *memère* and *pepère*. My grandparents. My father wasn't around much. Memère and pepère didn't like papa. They didn't say nice things about him. My mother always defended him, saying he was working hard to make a better life for us. She died in a car accident when I was three or four. Papa came, and I remember him crying at the funeral. That was my first real memory of him. My second was of a big fight he had with memère and pepère. Right after it, he took me away with him and I never saw them again. But for the next few years, every year, we'd go back to the cemetery where maman was buried. He'd stand at the grave and he'd cry. I hated it. I asked him why he came if it made him so sad. He told me he wasn't sad, he was angry. He said maman abandoned him and he couldn't forgive her for it." She spoke to his throat. He heard the slight hitch in her voice, a very faint tremor. Then it strengthened. "I know my father is a weak man, Garrett. But I can't abandon him, too. He'd never forgive me for it, any more than he forgave my mother."

There had to be some reason for these revelations. He remained silent, waiting. Her body against his was no longer limp and satisfied, but stiff with tension. He hoped she wasn't about to ask him for favors on her father's behalf. He wouldn't do any, and he refused to mislead her about it.

"I have something to tell you," she said.

He'd suspected as much. When he'd stopped to examine the day, it became clear to him that she hadn't been herself since she'd left the Access Nova Scotia office that morning, although she'd hidden it well. But there'd been a distant look in her eyes at lunch. She'd practically run through the pharmacy, and after their recent activities, he could attest that her need for feminine products hadn't been that urgent. She also already had a full box stashed in her bathroom. It had been nothing more than an excuse for her to go into the store alone. He wondered what she'd really purchased, and if that was what she was about to tell him. His mind raced with possibilities.

Then he had it. Thanks to the interesting conversation the children had initiated, he'd been distracted when she'd come back to the van after her test. She and her father were both runners, something she'd told him they used to do together. The stranger this morning had passed her a note with the URL for a running website on it, and he'd missed the significance. A running website would have particular meaning for her. He'd been jealous, rather than suspicious, that another man had passed her what he'd assumed was a phone number. Instead, she'd received a second message from her father. It was his fault for not picking up on it sooner.

He continued to wait, allowing her to gather her thoughts uninterrupted, until he feared she'd decided not to say anything more.

"Is it about the note you were passed this morning?" he finally prompted her. "The website was a message from your father, wasn't it?"

She lifted her head to look at him. In the pale moonlight washing the room, the dark pools of her eyes seemed to fill her face. Satiny strands of hair had stuck to her cheek and he freed them with the tip of a finger, tucking the tress behind her ear. He ran his finger down the length of her throat and along her bare shoulder, waiting for her to respond.

"There's a broken hyperlink embedded in it. At some point in the next few weeks it'll go live," she said.

He made a mental note to look for more broken hyperlinks in the other websites she'd visited. "How did the messenger who passed you the note know where to find you this morning?"

"I'd rather not say."

"Then I'll have to do more guessing. You asked me about your driver's license the day of the barbecue. Did somebody there say something to you?"

"Maybe."

It was impossible for her to tell a successful lie when she was pressed against him the way she was. He could feel every untruth in the subtle shifts of tension rippling through her body. Besides, at the barbecue, she hadn't been out of his sight the entire time. She'd talked to no one he didn't know. It could only have happened sometime between then and...

This morning.

He pictured her standing in the kitchen, using the phone, making a call to find out what time she should show up to write her test. She'd had no real conversation with anyone. It had been a series of prompts, directing her to an automated recording.

For someone to know where she'd be, they'd have to be tapped into the phone line. Or have access to telephone records.

He considered the ramifications if either of those scenarios were the case. It would mean that someone with excellent connections was in contact with Beausejour. But who would be willing to do him a personal favor of this magnitude?

The answer was no one. Not if Beausejour was simply a small link in a long chain.

There was nothing like stark reality to ruin an otherwise pleasant evening. He draped his arm over his eyes so he could think without giving anything away. He didn't understand her motives. He had no firm idea of her true level of involvement in her father's activities other than what she chose to tell him. He was becoming too emotionally invested, particularly since she'd repeatedly stated her loyalty was to her father—which meant sleeping together had been an error in judgment on both their parts. He didn't regret it. Not yet. But one of them was going to end up feeling used.

He concentrated on the fact that she'd made the attempt to warn him the telephone had been tapped. He had a greater problem, however. He didn't know who he could tell about this. He trusted his director.

He didn't trust whoever his director might be reporting to.

"You realize how serious this is, don't you?" he asked.

"Of course I do. So you should understand why I can't stay here any longer." She pushed off him, rolling to her hip and sitting upright on the edge of the bed before swinging her feet to the floor in a single graceful movement. "Find a different prison for me."

As she bent down to retrieve her shirt from the floor, the fall of her hair hid her face from his view. He caught a handful of it, combing his fingers through the silky strands. He couldn't understand how he'd ever thought she was plain. Her beauty was in both the uniform simplicity of her appearance and the depth and complexity of her quiet personality.

"You're not a prisoner," he said.

"No?" She scraped her hair out of his grasp and drew on her T-shirt, then flipped her long locks free of the collar. Her raised eyebrows and straight lips expressed her skepticism far better than mere words.

If she truly knew nothing, then none of this was her fault. If she turned out to be more actively involved, it was best if he didn't make too much out of it. Whoever had accessed the phone line didn't need any warning that they'd been found out.

He stretched out fully naked, twined his fingers together behind his head, and grinned at her as if he had no worries, either. "Well. Maybe you are. But only unofficially. You got a problem with that?"

Her eyes tracked the length of him. She trailed her fingertips from beneath one of his nipples to the curl of hair at his groin. "I don't want to cause problems for Peter and Cheryl."

He caught her hand and held it cupped in his against his abdomen. "It was Peter's decision to have you here.

He hired you. He's paying you. He has no one to blame but himself if it causes him problems."

She curled her fingers inside his palm, making a small fist. "What just happened between us," she began, a frown in her eyes. "What we did… Where do we go from here?"

"Would you like it to go somewhere?"

"I don't think it can."

So she understood the problems, too. "Why don't we just see where it leads us?"

She leaned forward to press her lips to his. He inhaled the feminine scent of her, reminded of her mouth on his body, and of hers beneath his. She straightened, then stepped away. He released her hand with reluctance.

"I should be going. It's late and I want to run in the morning," she said.

He didn't want her to leave. Once she stepped through the door, things would be different. She'd have regrets. So would he. "I can think of better ways to get exercise."

"I'm sure you can." She dragged her shorts up the long length of her legs. At the door to his bedroom, she paused. "I wish I could help you," she said softly, "but I can't."

She wasn't talking about exercise. Or sex.

He stared at the ceiling for a long time after she left, wishing he could believe with one hundred percent conviction that she couldn't help him because she didn't know anything.

CHAPTER TEN

IT WAS SATURDAY MORNING. The men had taken the children to the farm for a few hours, so the two women were changing the linen on all the beds and doing some cleaning. Rain pitter-pattered against the windowpanes.

"Have you given any thought to what you might do at the end of the summer?" Cheryl asked.

Isabelle snapped the freshly laundered sheet and watched it float into place on top of Kiefer's red Corvette toddler bed. Everyone seemed so concerned about her future. She was too, but she preferred not to think too hard about it. It loomed before her, a frightening, empty abyss. "I'll most likely try to find another family who wants to go abroad."

"Or, if you'd like," Cheryl said, a little too casually, "I can help you find work here, in the city. You're French, and fluent in four languages. You're also well-traveled. There are all kinds of government jobs for translators. Garrett and Peter could both find you something, too. Or, I could get you into one of the universities here if you'd prefer to go back to school. I know people in admissions." She smiled at Isabelle. "Peter and I were talking about helping you with the fees. You could spend your holidays here with us."

Isabelle was touched. The Mansfords were nice people. Too nice. Despite their impressive careers, they were both so naïve about the world at large. They could have no true idea of the life she'd led, or what she might be involved in, because if they did, they'd never make such an offer. She wasn't the most reliable person for them to invest in. She knew her own failings. Partway through the school year, she might decide to head off to Milan. Or London. Or back to Southeast Asia. Even she didn't know what she might do next.

She liked it that way. She might be tired of the uncertainty regarding her father, but she'd never grow weary of exploring life. It was one reason she enjoyed children so much. For them, every day was a new adventure.

"That's very kind of you," she said. "It's something for me to think about."

They moved on to Beth's room. Isabelle made the bed while Cheryl gathered the toys and put them back where they belonged so she could dust and vacuum.

Cheryl inserted a book onto a shelf with its companions. "You and Garrett seem to be hitting it off."

Isabelle's hand stilled for a split second as she was tucking a sheet corner under the mattress. She'd thought they'd been discreet. Garrett had been quite good at acting as if nothing intimate had happened between them.

A little too good.

"The children love him. I can see why he's a favorite of theirs," she said carefully.

Cheryl turned to face her. "I don't have any objections to you forming a friendship with my brother," she said. "It's obvious he's interested in you."

Isabelle could hardly deny that he was. She was interested in him, too. But it was far more complicated than his sister knew. Their lives had only gotten tangled together because of her father. Under normal circumstances, Garrett would never have noticed her. She was a puzzle to him. He wasn't nearly as much of a mystery to her. His work was his life.

"Your brother is bored and I'm a diversion," she replied.

Cheryl picked up the dust cloth and began wiping the furniture. "I'd like to think he has more substance to him than that."

"I didn't mean to imply otherwise. All I meant was that we spend a great deal of time together because of the children. He loves them a lot and enjoys their company, but sometimes it's nice for him to have another adult to talk to through the day, when you aren't here."

"I'll admit I'm a little disappointed. I thought maybe you and he were more serious than that," Cheryl said.

"I doubt very much if Garrett is ever serious about women. He likes his work too much. He likes the travel involved. He knows I understand that."

"You're one of the few women who do. That's why I'd hoped... Never mind."

Uneasiness prodded Isabelle. She had told Garrett she didn't want to cause problems for Peter and Cheryl. She'd meant over whatever was happening with her father, and the Mansfords' phone line being tapped. But she didn't want to create problems for him with his family either, and Cheryl had noticed his interest in her. She didn't want his sister to discover it involved his work, which he no doubt wished to keep separate from them.

"Garrett's not interested in forming a serious

relationship," she said. "Not at this point in his life, and certainly not with me."

Cheryl paused in the middle of dusting the top of Beth's pink dresser. She looked at Isabelle. "Why not with you?"

She hadn't expected to be asked to explain. She'd thought the answer self-evident. She could feel her cheeks burning. "I'm hardly his type."

"I'm not sure I agree with you. The last two women he was friends with weren't his type—which was precisely the reason they were nothing more than friends to him." Cheryl smiled. "Well. Maybe they were a little more. But you know what I mean."

Yes. And it wasn't something she particularly wished to hear about.

They finished cleaning the children's bedrooms. Isabelle moved on to her own while Cheryl took care of hers and Peter's.

Upstairs, Isabelle left a stack of clean bedding in Garrett's suite for him. As she was making her bed, her fingers touched the cell phone she'd tucked under her mattress. She hadn't yet checked the running website.

She couldn't ignore it forever. She picked up her laptop and sat on the sofa. The screen flickered to life. Within a few minutes, she was checking the hyperlinks. None were broken. That meant she had to check each of them.

By the third, she'd found what she needed—a string of digits that contained a phone number for her to call. The country code was Belgian. She recognized it from a few years ago, when they'd lived in a little town not far from the French border.

That didn't mean he was in Belgium.

She checked the rest of the links to cover her tracks.

Then, she shut down the laptop and stared at the phone. She wanted—desperately—to hear her father's voice. Once she called him, however, she'd be making a choice and there'd be no turning back from it. She knew Garrett wasn't foolish enough to trust her, but this would be crossing the fine line they'd established. There'd be no more friendship between them. Not of any kind.

Quickly, before she changed her mind, she punched in the numbers.

"*Allo?*"

"Papa?" He sounded so familiar. So *normal*. Her hands were shaking. Her lungs refused to expand as all of the anxiety she'd suffered over the past few months, all her worry for him, struck her full force. "Where have you *been*?"

"*Ma Belle*. I can't talk long. I've been working. I'm sorry I missed you in Thailand, but it couldn't be helped. I'll make it up to you, I promise. Right now, you'll have to be patient."

It would serve no purpose to be angry with him. He had no idea she'd been left stranded and penniless while she'd waited. She'd rather find out what was happening with him. She wanted Garrett to be *wrong*.

"Where are you? What can I do?" she asked.

"It's best if you don't know where I am just yet. There's nothing you can do except wait to hear from me again. Well," he amended. "The work I'm doing right now... It's more sensitive than usual. I can't afford for the wrong people to learn of it. I need to know if anyone's been asking you questions about me."

She heard an unfamiliar edge in his voice. Or, perhaps, for the first time, she knew what to listen for. For years, she'd shrugged off his penchant for drama as being part of who he was. It had always seemed harmless to her. Like a game only the two of them shared. Now, she was no longer as certain. "Why would anyone be asking me questions?"

"When security management is involved, it's impossible to be too careful. People's lives are at stake."

She wanted so much to believe in him. "How did you find out where I am?"

If he heard the suspicion in her question, he ignored it. "I have friends in the right places. Don't worry, darling. As usual, you'll simply have to trust me. I love you."

"I love you, too."

Her father disconnected the call. Isabelle sat for a long time, listening to the sound of the rain on the windows and the roof.

That was the problem. She loved her father, but she didn't trust him anymore. And it was very difficult to have one without the other.

Garrett told Peter he suspected his phone was being tapped.

Peter, in typical fashion, shrugged it off. "These things are bound to happen when you have a spy in the family. I'll tell Cheryl to keep her business calls to her cell phone."

Peter assumed it was something CSIS had done, and Garrett left it at that, even though they both knew full well that CSIS had no legal right to spy on Canadian citizens. Not on Canadian soil. But he saw no need to drag Isabelle into this. It wasn't her fault.

What he should have done, however, was to call his director and tell him, too. He didn't. He'd rather discuss his concerns about a possible leak in the department in private, when he knew for certain they wouldn't be overheard. That meant a trip to Ottawa was in order.

He booked a flight for Monday, then spent Saturday morning in the barns with the children, out of the rain. He helped Chelsea bottle-feed a calf. Beth had abandoned them for her aunt's kitchen, where they were baking cookies. Kiefer had the kittens to occupy him. At coffee time, Garrett sat down with Peter, his nephews, and the hired hands.

All the time, he worried about what Isabelle might be doing. He disliked having her out of his sight for any length of time, and not only because he didn't trust her. She both fascinated and frustrated him. He'd been far more open with her than she'd been with him. Despite everything they'd done together—talking and otherwise— there was a part of her he hadn't been able to touch. Because she didn't trust him, either.

They returned to the house for lunch. Afterward, Peter settled in the family room with the children to watch a movie. Before Garrett could suggest he take Isabelle for a drive, Cheryl cornered him.

"Why don't you and I go grab a coffee?" she suggested. "There's a little coffee shop in town I don't get to visit nearly often enough. We could have some sibling alone time. I don't get nearly enough of that, either."

He couldn't say no. He loved his sister. Both of them, in fact. Besides, she was right and he wasn't about to pass up an opportunity to be alone with one of them.

The farm sat on the outskirts of a small town. The coffee shop nestled near its center, in the main shopping area, between a shoe store and an exclusive women's boutique. The main street and sidewalk were constructed of brick, giving the district a distinct European vibe. The buildings were all heritage. Garrett parked in a lot behind the shops. Sharing an umbrella, he and his sister dashed through a short alley.

The coffee shop was full when they entered and they had to wait a few minutes for a table. Finally, however, they found a spot in the middle, between what Garrett surmised was a grad student working on a research paper, judging by the stack of books and the open laptop, and two elderly ladies who'd been shopping. The two empty chairs at their table were piled high with bags.

"So," Garrett said, taking a sip of his coffee. It was fair trade, black and bold, and very good. The atmosphere in the shop was decent, too. Warm and relaxed. Not much wonder Cheryl liked to come here without the children. "What did you want to talk about that you didn't want Peter to overhear?"

Cheryl laughed. "Am I that obvious?"

"Yes. You're a good lawyer. You'd suck at espionage." He took a shot in the dark. "It's about Isabelle, isn't it?"

"I really am obvious." She smiled at him. "So are you. You like her."

His stomach dropped. His sister planned to play matchmaker. While not entirely unexpected, this was the last thing he needed. Peter would kill him if he misled Cheryl by raising her hopes. He wouldn't do it, anyway.

"I find her interesting, yes." That was the truth. "She's different from most women." Also true.

"You're over thirty." Cheryl plowed on. "You might want to start thinking about your future."

His first inclination was to laugh. "Are you seriously giving me a big sister talk about relationships with women?"

"It's more along the lines of me being worried about

you. You don't have a home. You spend most of your time out of the country. I know all that's exciting right now, and I'm not suggesting you give it up, but at some point, you're going to realize you've missed opportunities that have nothing to do with your career. There aren't too many women who'd enjoy the kind of lifestyle you lead. Not fulltime. I'd hate for you to end up lonely and alone because you were too focused on work."

Her words stung more than they should. The conversation no longer seemed funny. He tried to steer it away from becoming too serious. "I'll have you know, your nieces think I'm quite a catch."

"You are." Cheryl's hazel eyes met his over the rim of the coffee mug she cradled in both hands. "But so is Isabelle. And the truth is, even though I love you, you're a bit of an ass when it comes to women."

That was downright insulting. "Women love me."

"Because you're a challenge. They like that. Right up until they figure out how much work it really takes to keep you interested in them. Name the last time you were the one to break off a relationship with a woman. Then tell me the last time you were sorry it happened." He had no answers for her and she knew it, so she forged ahead. "You don't trust people, Garrett. You're very secretive about your life, even with family. And I think you're recognizing those same qualities in Isabelle. That's why you find her so interesting."

He had a sudden tingle of disquiet. His sister was more right than he liked. He and Isabelle did share those same qualities. The difference, however, was that Isabelle saw right through him. He was no challenge to her.

He said nothing. Cheryl, for her part, was far from finished. "In some ways, I think you're all wrong for her. She's too serious for her age and you can be far too intense. But in other ways, the ones that matter, I think she's perfect. She understands you far better than anyone else you've shown this much interest in ever did." She set down her mug. "You might be missing an opportunity with her you'll someday regret."

His sister was under so many misconceptions. He wasn't missing any opportunity by choice, but through necessity. "Why are you assuming I'm the one playing hard to get?" he asked. "The truth is, Isabelle knows what she wants. I'm not it."

In seconds, Cheryl's surprise turned to sympathy.

"I'm so sorry," she said.

"So am I." He was. He was sorry that Isabelle's loyalties lay with a father who didn't deserve them. And he felt terrible that his sister was looking at him the way she was, as if she believed his heart had been broken. He hadn't been stupid enough to allow his feelings for Isabelle to go that far.

He hadn't.

Cheryl knew when to retreat. They talked about other things as they finished their coffee. Their sister had taken a new position with a brokerage firm. Their parents were considering selling the family business, a decision they'd all been hoping for. At this point in their lives, they should be thinking about retirement.

After coffee, he followed his sister as she ducked into a few neighboring stores. On the one hand, it was nice to be out of Isabelle's company for a few hours. When she wasn't around, he could think with far more objectivity. On the other, however, curiosity over what she was doing consumed him. She was turning into an obsession, and he didn't like it—or what it said about him. His interest in her activities had very little to do with his current case.

By the time they returned home, the movie was over

and Peter had fallen asleep on the sofa in the family room. Isabelle was in the kitchen with the children. Kiefer was painting with watercolors on a long strip of brown freezer paper she'd fastened to the back of a closet door. The girls were making jewelry from beads at the granite island.

"Doesn't this look like fun!" Cheryl exclaimed, hanging her wet raincoat on a hook by the entry. "Mind if I join you?"

Isabelle looked up. Her gaze collided with Garrett's over the tops of the girls' heads. And he discovered she wasn't as much of a mystery to him as he'd thought. Something had happened. She glanced away far too quickly.

"This would be a good time for your first driving lesson. How about it?" he asked her.

He thought she might refuse. Instead, she slid off her stool and offered the empty to seat to Cheryl. "Let me get my jacket."

Garrett watched her leave the room. The hem of her short skirt floated around her long legs with each sensual movement of her hips.

Cheryl picked up the bag of beads and emptied a few into her palm. Her tone dripped with disapproval, tempered by a touch of concern. "I hope you know what you're doing."

He did. He wished he didn't.

"Slow down. There's a sharp turn coming up. Just past it, I want you to take the first road to the right."

Isabelle eased her foot off the gas and gently applied the brakes. Garrett was proving to be a patient instructor.

They'd practiced backing up in the driveway a few times before he'd allowed her to take the van on the road.

She tried to focus on her driving, but worry made it hard. Eventually, he'd get to the real reason he'd offered to give her a lesson and the suspense was killing her. He couldn't possibly know about the telephone call, although she half hoped he did. It would make everything so much easier for her. She wouldn't have this awful sense of being torn in two very different directions.

The rain had turned to a soft mist. Fields, lush and green with thigh-high corn, gave way to forest. Past the turn was the road he'd told her to expect, partially hidden between the trees. It was gravel on the surface, yet slick with mud underneath from the rain. The tires slid a little when she pressed too heavily on the accelerator. She overcompensated by hitting the brakes too hard. Rocks spun off the tires. They lurched forward against their seat belts as the van shuddered to a halt.

"Sorry," she said, her knuckles white on the steering wheel. "I didn't expect it to be so slippery."

"You're doing fine. This is close to how slush and snow tug at the tires in winter. That was why I suggested you turn here. I thought it might be good for you to feel the difference. If you keep going," he pointed ahead through the intermittent slapping of the windshield wipers, "there's a place for you to turn around."

She inched the van forward, more cautious now. She saw the widened area on the side of the road he'd indicated. As she pulled the van into it, trying to make the turn in a half circle, the heavens opened. Buckets of water pounded off the roof of the van and streamed down the windshield, making it impossible for the wipers to keep up. She couldn't see a thing.

She stopped the van, afraid if she went ahead any

farther, she'd drive off the shoulder and into the woods. "What do I do?"

"Put it in park and shut off the engine. We'll sit here and wait for the rain to let up."

She managed the gearshift but fumbled with the unfamiliar ignition. Garrett reached over and helped her find the right position for the key, his hand swallowing hers. Her thoughts shifted to the way he'd pinned both of hers to his bed, and everything that followed. Each second of heart-pounding pleasure.

The rain continued to pour. The inside of the van became the entire world, and he filled every inch of it. She eased her fingers from beneath his touch.

He hadn't taken his eyes off her.

"You've been avoiding me," he said.

"And you've let me."

"No," he corrected her. "I've been giving you space. But something happened today. I'd like to know what it was."

Isabelle's mouth went dry, her heart hammering so loud she was certain he must hear it over the steady drumming of the rain. She'd made her decision. Now she had to live with it. She hadn't told her father that she believed CSIS was searching for him. She wasn't telling Garrett anything more than she already had, either. She didn't want to choose sides between them.

She turned her face away and looked at the streaming driver's side window so she wouldn't have to meet his eyes and read the disappointment in them. When she spoke, she was as honest with him as she could be. "I have nothing to tell you."

He cupped her chin in firm fingers and forced her to look at him. His expression was grave, but he'd shut down his thoughts so she couldn't read them. The creases around his mouth, so evident when he smiled, had smoothed. He dropped a light kiss on her lips.

"I guess this is it, then," he said.

She swallowed hard against the painful lump in her throat. She'd known from the beginning there could never be anything of significance between them. She hadn't expected to fall in love with him.

The rain slowed, then stopped altogether. The sun burst through a break in the clouds. Regret burned at the backs of her eyes. "I wish things could have been different."

He let go of her and settled back in the passenger seat, six feet of rugged male indifference wrapped in a white Henley shirt and wheat-colored Dockers.

"Put your right foot on the brake, start the engine, and slide the gearshift into drive," he said. "If you cut the wheels hard to the left, you should be able to pull back onto the road with no problem at all. Stay clear of the shoulder. It'll be soft."

Slowly, Isabelle maneuvered the van onto the dirt road. Muddy water from the puddles sprayed off the tires as she stepped on the accelerator. A minute later, they were on pavement again.

"For the record," Garrett said, staring straight ahead, "I wish things could have been different, too."

CHAPTER ELEVEN

GARRETT'S PLANE TOUCHED DOWN on the runway with a bump and the heavy exhalation of reverse thrusters. It taxied to the terminal. Ten minutes later, the seat belt lights blinked off and people crowded the narrow aisle, tugging their laptops and carry-ons from the overhead bins.

In front of the terminal, he grabbed a taxi for CSIS headquarters in Ottawa's East end. He had an evening flight back to Halifax to catch, even though there was no chance he'd be getting more information from Isabelle. She knew too much about him and who he worked for, and she was bent on protecting her father.

While he'd never intended to make her choose between them, he'd hoped she'd decide to do what was morally right. Isabelle, however, honestly wanted to believe that her father's activities were no more than a game and it wasn't Garrett's job to try to convince her otherwise. He dealt in information. Facts. All of which indicated Marc Beausejour was involved in something far bigger than CSIS had suspected.

The taxi pulled up at the entrance to a rectangular, concrete and glass building. Garrett paid the driver, then went through security. Once inside he headed straight for the director's office, pausing only to speak to a few people he knew. He took an elevator to a sunny office on the third floor. The office overlooked a row of cultivated trees and beyond it, the parking lot.

John Carmichael sat at his desk, a dark frown of concentration permanently etched on his face. Garrett guessed his age to be around sixty—maybe a little more, could be less. He was retired military, with an impressive career that spring-boarded off a degree in engineering from the prestigious Royal Military Academy. That was all his immediate staff knew of him, or at least, was willing to share. Garrett had never seen his wife, although John wore a ring so assumed he was married.

John looked up when he noticed Garrett standing in the doorway. "Have a seat, Downing. What's so important it couldn't wait one more week?"

"Isabelle Beausejour is a dead end," Garrett said. "She's not going to give up any information on her father. She knows what I am—and no, I didn't tell her. But from what little she's told me, Beausejour doesn't trust her any more than he does anyone else. He's got her convinced he's nothing more than a big kid playing high stakes poker."

"Aren't we all," John said. Garrett could hear the fatigue in his voice. "Is it worth bringing her in to see if maybe you've missed something?"

Garrett gave his honest opinion. "No. He hasn't involved her in anything. Not yet, anyway. I do think she can lead us to him, but your guess is as good as mine as to when that might be. He's hiding, and he's not telling her where." He cleared his throat. "There's a bigger reason I'm here. Beausejour has some serious connections. He managed to track down where Isabelle's been staying and tapped into my brother-in-law's home phone line."

John's jaw went slack. "You are shitting me."

"I wish I was."

Garrett filled him in.

The director slumped back in his chair. "Why am I just hearing about this now?"

"Because I wanted to tell you in private. If he could track down his daughter and tap a phone line, and hand deliver a message to her, all while hiding his physical location through a VPN, do you still think he's a little man?"

"No," John said. "I don't."

"So here's what we know. Beausejour's name has come up a few times in previous investigations dealing with stolen military goods. He grew up in Canada. He's got some good connections here. We also know that a Dutch player is close friends with our minister of National Defence, and also happens to be a friend of Beausejour's. The minister has lots of friends we don't know about. If we connect the dots, who do you suppose one of those friends might be? Who's our best guess?"

"It's going to take a lot more than my best guess to make me start pointing fingers at the minister," John said.

"But is it enough to make you withhold a few details in your reports to him?"

"Yes." John rubbed the back of his neck, admitting defeat. "It is. Let's back up and go over what we know about Beausejour's personal life for a minute. He has a daughter, also born in Canada. His wife died in a car accident. She and the daughter were living in northern Quebec with her parents at the time. Do we know if he has any remaining immediate family other than the daughter?"

"None that we've found. Isabelle doesn't seem to

know anything about her family here. She was too young when she left Canada to remember much. She said her grandparents never liked her father, and they had a fight with him after her mother's funeral. The next day, he took her away and she never saw them again."

John tapped his chin with steepled fingers, thinking over everything Garrett said. Garrett could see the wheels spinning.

"Find the grandparents," John finally said. "Ask a few questions. If they didn't like him, they must have had a good reason."

Garrett canceled his flight to Halifax and booked one for Quebec City instead. From there he rented a car and drove for seven hours to a small town called Lac Saint-Pierre.

He checked in at the first motel he found. It was late at night and the young man at the desk spoke very little English. While Garrett's French was excellent, the sullen teenager claimed to have difficulty understanding him. Since all Garrett wanted from him was a room to sleep in, that point wasn't too hard to get across.

GPS got him to Isabelle's grandparents' house the next morning.

Their white clapboard, two-story house sat off the main road at the end of a long, narrow dirt driveway. Trees surrounded the two-acre property. The large lawn had been neatly trimmed. The smell of fresh-cut grass flowed through his open car window. Two enormous flowerbeds fronted the house. A stone walkway led to the main door.

M. and Mme. Anjelais turned out to be a lovely couple

who had no trouble understanding his French. Garrett liked them at once. While Isabelle looked nothing like her slight, white-haired grandmother, the two women shared mannerisms that he found uncanny. A graceful tilt of the head. A quiet, rapt intentness when something caught their attention.

He'd captured Mme. Anjelais's with his first words.

"I'm a friend of Isabelle Beausejour," he said after introducing himself. "I'm searching for her grandparents."

M. Anjelais recovered first. He opened the screen door wide. "Perhaps you should come in."

Garrett was ushered into a bright front room flooded with morning sunshine. It held a piano in one corner, an overstuffed pink sofa, and two matching armchairs. He took one of the chairs beside the lace-adorned window. The older couple shared the sofa facing him.

Mme. Anjelais's eyes were anxious. "What is Isabelle like?" she asked. "Is she happy? Has Leon been good to her?"

So, they knew Beausejour as Leon, too.

Garrett could only imagine their fears. He did what he could to alleviate them. "She's wonderful," he assured her. "She works as an au pair. Very quiet, but she can take care of herself. Nothing much seems to bother her."

Mme. Anjelais's eyes misted over. "She's like her mother, then. Christelle had a quiet personality. Everyone loved her."

They talked for some time. Garrett answered what questions he could. He'd come here to get information, not give it, however, and it made him uncomfortable to be raising these peoples' hopes of a reunion when he wasn't certain how Isabelle would feel about it. He doubted if Beausejour would have painted what little memory she had of them with a flattering brush.

"If you don't mind me asking," he said, "how did your daughter meet Isabelle's father?"

"At university," M. Anjelais replied. "They both went to McGill in Montreal. Christelle planned to become a doctor. All of that ended when she met Leon, though. The next thing we knew she was pregnant and they were getting married."

The Defence minister had gone to McGill, too. It would be a simple matter to check dates to see if they were there together. Yearbooks were another good source of information.

"They must have had mutual friends."

"Leon was friends with anyone who mattered. He had a talent for identifying people who were going to be successful. I think that was why Christelle interested him so much. Everyone liked her. People liked Leon, too."

"But you didn't like him."

"No," M. Anjelais admitted. "Because we saw what he did to Christelle. The lies he told her. The promises he made to her, and to Isabelle, that he never kept. He was difficult to say no to. He used everyone he met. He borrowed money that he never repaid. Twice we had people come here to collect."

Garrett filed that away as information worth investigating. Even back then, Beausejour had a pattern of narcissistic, entitled behavior. "Did he have any family?"

"Only his mother. She loved him, but she made no excuses for him. We kept in touch with her, hoping he'd bring Isabelle to visit her at least, but he never did. She passed away a few years ago."

Garrett was forming a very clear picture of Isabelle's father. It came as no great shock, but it didn't fit the image she had of him at all.

"When do we get to meet Isabelle?" Mme. Anjelais asked.

That was the question he'd been dreading to hear. But it wouldn't matter if Isabelle were angry with him for coming here. These people deserved to know their only grandchild and Isabelle was too kind to disappoint them by refusing.

"She doesn't know I came to see you. I wanted to make sure I had the right people before I told her. Why don't you give me a few days?" he suggested. "I'll give her your phone number and she can call you when she's ready."

"Does she remember us at all?"

The wistful longing in Mme. Anjelais's voice made Garrett feel like the worst kind of exploiter. He wished he'd come here with better, more honorable intentions. The least he could offer her was honesty and hope.

"She does. She remembers her mother, too," he said. He rose to leave. He had a long drive ahead of him and an early morning flight to catch. "Don't worry. She'll call you."

He'd see that she did.

The seven hour drive back to Quebec City left him with plenty of time to think. He'd gotten far too close to Isabelle. He cared too much that she would be hurt. He'd get nothing more from her, nor did he wish to. Not the way things now stood between them. He had other trails to follow in order to recover the missing DND weapons systems parts, the real focus of his investigation. Beausejour was only one of them.

The thought of parting from Isabelle tore a raw, jagged hole in his chest—one that would only get bigger as the days passed if he wasn't careful.

It was time to let her go.

He would report to the director first thing in the morning to let him know what little he'd learned from the grandparents, and tell him that he was ready to explore other leads.

Isabelle stood in the center of the Mansfords' kitchen and tried to process what Garrett was saying to her.

The children were in the family room, playing a video game with friends. Cheryl and Peter were both in the city, working. Isabelle had been making lunch when Garrett arrived at the door.

He'd been gone for three days. She'd missed him far more than was wise.

Until this second.

"What do you mean—you paid a visit to my grandparents? Why would you do that? Never mind," she answered herself. "Did you find out anything of use to your investigation from them?"

He had the decency to look at least a little ashamed. When he spoke, however, he sounded anything but. His voice became very quiet.

"I'm not going to apologize for doing my job. And if, in doing my job, one decent thing comes out of the mess your father created, I'm going to be glad for it." She flinched at the rebuke. "They're decent people, Isabelle. For twenty years, they've worried about what might have happened to you. Try to imagine how that must have been for them. The least you can do is let them know you're okay."

She knew she should have contacted them long before now. The truth was, however, she'd thought very little about them over the years. The bits and pieces of memory she'd once had of them had faded a long time ago. It was the slight against her father that couldn't go unchallenged.

"My grandparents had no love for my father," she said, slicing a tomato for sandwiches with meticulous care. "I don't remember a lot about those days, but I do recall them telling him to get out and never come back. If there is a mess, it was created by everyone, not only him."

Garrett didn't argue the point, which only served to anger her further. She didn't want him to be right. It would mean that so much about her life was all wrong. She laid the tomato on bread, then added slices of roast beef and cheese. She had no idea whose fault it was that she'd never been allowed to return to visit them. Her grandparents might have told him to get out, but she couldn't remember if they'd told him to take her, too.

Garrett placed an envelope on the kitchen island beside the cutting board. "Your grandmother sent you a note. It includes their contact information. At least let them know you're okay," he repeated.

He picked up his overnight bag and left the room. She could hear his footsteps on the stairs.

She fingered the envelope, tapping it against the granite countertop. She wasn't so certain she really was okay.

Garrett sat down with Peter that evening in his office. They had a few matters to discuss.

"My vacation's been cut short. I'm leaving tomorrow," he said.

This was a familiar routine and Peter didn't ask where

he was going. The leather wingback chair creaked as he pushed away from his desk. "What happens with Isabelle at the end of the summer? Did you want me to find other work for her? Or are you no longer keeping an eye on her?"

"I won't be," Garrett said. "I can't speak for anyone else." He drummed his fingers on the armrest of his chair. He couldn't leave without knowing she was taken care of, or at least that he'd done his best for her. Memories of Bangkok, and her situation there, remained too firmly fixed in his head. "I'm not sure what she wants to do."

"Cheryl offered to help her get into a university," Peter said. "She said she'd think about it."

She was being polite. Based on their past conversation, he didn't believe she had any real interest in it. "She can't afford it, and she'll never get a student loan. She hasn't lived in the country for years."

Peter smoothed his fingers along the edge of his desk. "I'm willing to lend her the money."

Garrett was uncomfortably reminded that his family knew very little about Isabelle and her circumstances. The minute she heard from her father, she'd be gone. "When I first asked you to find work for her, I never meant for you to take her on as a full-time responsibility," he said carefully. "Lending her money might not be a good investment."

Peter's eyebrows shot up. "Really. And you know this because…?"

"It's complicated." Garrett shifted in his seat, trying to find the right words to say without giving too much away. He gave up. "Look. If she wants to go to university, I'll give you the money to lend her. That way if she suddenly decides school's not for her, you aren't on the hook for it."

"I don't care about the money."

Garrett didn't, either. It was more the principle that bothered him, because he hadn't been upfront with Peter. For that matter, neither had Isabelle. "You're too trusting."

"And you aren't trusting enough." Peter leaned forward. "You think I don't know that she has to be involved in something significant for you to be watching her so closely? I can figure out some things on my own. From where I'm sitting, I don't think she's done anything wrong. She's more likely a victim of circumstances. Otherwise, she'd have been arrested. Personally, I'd rather give her the benefit of the doubt and be proven right than assume the worst and be proven wrong. You should try it sometime. You'd make more friends that way."

Garrett didn't dare give her the benefit of any doubt because he didn't want to be disappointed in her. He didn't want her to be disappointed in him, either. Right now, they understood each other.

"Fine. I'll try your approach. Let me front the money for any university fees. But do me a favor. Don't tell her it's from me. She can owe the money to you."

"You're such an idiot," Peter said with a sigh. "I told you to leave her alone but you wouldn't listen to me."

He hadn't needed any warnings. He'd known better from the very beginning. It simply hadn't stopped him.

"You told me not to use her to get information. I didn't." He stood. "I've got to go pack. I need to say good-bye to the kids, too."

He helped Cheryl tuck the children in bed. She stopped him in the hall and beckoned him into her bedroom. She shut the door behind them.

"Why are you really leaving?" she asked. "You still

have another week of vacation. It's because of Isabelle, isn't it?"

"It's really not," he replied. "Duty calls. I'll get to make up the vacation time later." She looked so worried it made him laugh. "Quit being such a big sister," he teased her. "I don't have a broken heart."

"Maybe not broken." She wrapped her arms around him and gave him a hard hug. "More like bruised. It serves you right, too. It had to happen sooner or later."

He hugged her back. "Can you do me one favor? Isabelle doesn't really have anyone she can count on. Can you keep an eye on her? And let me know if she needs anything?"

"You mean, be a big sister to her instead of you?"

"Something like that."

"Of course I will," Cheryl said. "I like her." She kissed his cheek. "But I love you."

Isabelle stood in the hall outside Garrett's door. He was leaving. She'd heard him say good-bye to the children.

It was obvious he had no intention of saying good-bye to her.

Whatever his reasons had been for visiting her grandparents, she should have thanked him. The phone call to them had been far easier than she'd expected. They'd been so happy to hear from her. But it was difficult for her to reconcile the cold-hearted man they said had taken their grandchild from them with the warm, loving person who'd raised her. It was as if he were two separate people. One of them was a complete stranger to her.

She took a deep breath and knocked on the door.

"Come in."

He was standing by the window, gazing into the night. He still had on the dress shirt and trousers he'd arrived in that morning, although he'd removed the tie and his collar was open. He looked...unwelcoming. Not at all like the same man she'd made love with only a few days ago.

She didn't enter the room but remained in the security of the open doorway. She hadn't been especially friendly to him that morning either, so she had no right to judge.

"I heard that you're leaving," she said. "I wanted to thank you before you go. For everything, but especially for giving me my grandparents' telephone number. I called them this evening. They sound very nice."

"They are." He said nothing more than that.

Tiny fingers plucked at her heart. She should go. It was obvious he wanted nothing more to do with her. They'd already said everything, anyway. She wavered, half turning to leave, then stopped and turned back.

"Is there any way at all I can leave you with a better impression of me than the one I've made?" she asked quietly.

His expression thawed. His eyes zeroed in on her face. "You have no idea the kind of impression you've made on me. There's certainly no need for you to worry that it's bad."

"Thank you." She started to close the door.

"Isabelle."

She stopped. A spark of hope kindled to life. "Yes?"

"I'm no longer investigating your father. That doesn't mean he isn't still under investigation. You should be careful."

The spark died. "I understand."

"And Isabelle?" He crossed the room to the door in a

few long strides. He gave her a quick, fierce kiss. "If you ever need anything—if you're ever in trouble again, like in Bangkok—Cheryl will know how to reach me. Stay in touch with her."

She nodded without speaking, then returned to her own suite of rooms. She closed the door and leaned against it, squeezing her eyes tightly shut. Her whole life was a lie. One would think she'd have learned to keep her heart to herself.

Instead, she'd fallen for a man who lied for a living.

CHAPTER TWELVE

Halifax, Nova Scotia, late November

ISABELLE CROSSED COBURG ROAD onto Chestnut Street, then cut down Payzant to the old townhouse on the corner where she shared an apartment with three other girls. The icy November wind off the harbor seeped through the seams of the fleece-lined denim jacket she wore. Winter was here. She'd need to invest in heavier clothing.

She clattered up the slick wooden front steps, unlocked the door, and ducked into the small entry. In front of her was the door to the laundry room they shared with the two other apartments in the building. To her left was a flight of stairs. She kicked off her boots and dashed up the stairs to her apartment.

No one else was home. She breathed a small sigh of relief. They were nice enough roommates, but she wasn't used to sharing her personal space and one girl, Talia, invited her boyfriend over to spend the night far too often. The walls were thin.

Isabelle's bedroom was at the end of a narrow hall, next to the living room and opposite the kitchen. The other three bedrooms were on the third floor of the building. She hung her jacket on a hook beside the stairwell and carried her book bag to her bedroom, where she dropped it in a corner.

She flung herself face down on the narrow bed. She'd lived in worse places, but right now, she couldn't recall them. Summer and fall in Nova Scotia had both been beautiful, but winter was getting off to a shaky start in her books. It was dark, dreary, and damply cold. She hated university, too. While her marks were good, she simply didn't care for the structure. And the thought of living four or five years in the same place was almost unbearable.

She'd had a few website messages from her father that all was well, but busy, and she couldn't help thinking that things weren't well with her, yet that didn't seem to hold any significance for him. He loved her. She knew it. But at some point, he'd stopped caring about her.

She'd been abandoned.

By Garrett, too. She hadn't heard from him since August. That was also unbearable. Maybe even more so. She still spoke with Cheryl Mansford on a regular basis— she owed the Mansfords so much money it gave her heart palpitations to think about it—but Cheryl never had too much to say about her brother, and Isabelle wouldn't ask. She'd learned he was in New Delhi with the High Commission of Canada. That was it. She'd finally had to accept that it really had been her father he was interested in. This foolish ache in her heart would heal given time.

She lifted her head and glanced at the clock. She had a half hour before heading to work. The city was an international port and one of the taverns on the waterfront had been thrilled to hire her when they found out she spoke four languages. Sailors proved to be good tippers and she needed the money.

Half an hour later, freezing in the ultrashort Nova Scotia tartan mini-kilt that was part of her uniform, she wrestled through the heavy wooden doors of the tavern.

Inside, despite the blustery weather, the atmosphere was warm and welcoming. Stout oak rafters braced the low ceiling. Hand-carved tables with benches instead of chairs, also solid oak, formed a wide column down the center of the room, facing a small stage for the band. To the right was the bar. A second room, beyond the first, held booths for people more interested in eating than drinking and listening to music. The stone slab floor kept the smell of stale beer to a breathable level. And she had to admit, the no smoking policy in the province made the air quality a vast improvement over many of the European pubs she'd been in.

She left her jacket and boots in the back, slipped her shoes on, and grabbed a round brass tray from a shelf on the way to her section. Jack, one of the bartenders, waved to her as she passed by. He was cute, with spiky blond hair and vivid blue eyes that crinkled at the corners whenever he smiled, which was often. There was nothing mysterious about him. He studied biology at one of the universities. He'd asked her out three times now, and each time, she'd made an excuse, but it had been almost three months since she'd last seen Garrett.

It was time to move on.

She stopped in her tracks, spun so that the short, pleated kilt flared around her thighs, and went back to the bar. She set her tray on the polished counter. "Hey, Jack."

"Hey, Isabelle." His eyes smiled into hers, flirty and hopeful. "What's up?"

She waited for that little jolt she got in the pit of her stomach whenever Garrett looked at her that way, but it didn't happen. She felt herself frowning, then the first fingers of panic. She didn't understand. She liked Jack. He was cute, and friendly, and the other girls who worked here thought she was crazy for turning him down. She *wanted* to give him a chance. She'd made up her mind. *What are you doing Friday night?*

All she had to do was ask. But the words simply wouldn't come out.

He was staring at her now, the smile replaced with a look of concern. "Is something the matter?"

"I forget what I was going to say," she lied. "The cold must have numbed my brain on the walk to work."

His lips quirked upward. "I hate to be the one to break it to you, but this isn't cold. Technically, it's still the middle of fall. Winter's a month away."

"Do you kick puppies, too?" she asked. "And tell small children Santa Claus doesn't really exist?"

A grin crept across his face. "The naughty ones, yes."

Those icy fingers of panic lost some of their grip. *Go on. Ask him out*, her inner voice—the one with the common sense—urged her.

She couldn't do it. He was funny and nice. An open book. She had no trouble figuring out what he was thinking. And that was the problem. She wanted someone who challenged her. Who scattered her senses.

She wanted Garrett.

She couldn't see herself encouraging Jack when her thoughts were with another man—even one who hadn't spared her a second thought of his own since walking away.

She finished her shift. As she was slipping her arms into the sleeves of her jacket at the end of the night, preparing to leave, the cell phone in one of the pockets started to buzz, vibrating against her ribs. She carried it out of habit. She hadn't received a call on it since the summer. There was only one person who'd be contacting her now. No one else had the number.

She debated not answering, but in her heart, that was no real solution. She fumbled with the phone, flicking the ON button with a touch of her thumb. "Isabelle Beausejour."

"Belle, mon petit choux. Comment vas-tu?"

Garrett had asked to be sent to Amsterdam and been turned down. The director already had an intelligence officer in place.

He'd been sent to India instead.

"There's a lot more going on than a few missing aircraft parts," John had said to Garrett. "The RBN is a pain in my ass. Not to mention that other issue." He was referring to Vanderloord, the friend of the Minister of Defence, who also had a connection to Isabelle's father. "I want you to find out who in India is moving those weapons systems parts into Pakistan."

So here he was. He sipped at his champagne and tried his best not to look bored. Tonight, the High Commission of Canada in India was hosting a Christmas reception for ex-pats and business associates at its offices in New Delhi. The ex-pats didn't interest Garrett as much as a few of the other invitees—in particular, the three officials from the combined provinces of Jammu and Kashmir. The weapons systems parts were being routed through Kashmir into Pakistan. A Canadian ex-pat with connections to Amsterdam had been in Kashmir last month. Another one of those connections was Isabelle's father, who remained MIA.

His fingers tightened around the stem of the delicate crystal flute. Every day he fought the urge to call her, to see how she was doing. She was still in Nova Scotia, attending university. Peter kept him up to date, but not without disapproval.

"I don't like her thinking she owes us money," Peter had said during their last phone conversation. "You paid her tuition, not us."

"Tell her it's a gift and that she should pay it forward someday."

"Not everyone likes handouts, Garrett. She's not a charity case. She's young, and having a run of bad luck, and could use some direction—something she's never had, if I'm guessing correctly."

Garrett could literally feel the censure seeping through the phone connection. He sighed. "Make arrangements with her to pay it back, but in small increments."

She'd eventually forget about the money. Her attitude toward it was cavalier at best. He didn't really believe she'd stay in school for four years either, given her initial lack of enthusiasm for the idea, but he figured his investment would at least keep her occupied until she made some firm decisions about her life. It also gave her the opportunity to cut all ties with her father. Time would tell.

Does she ever ask about me?

He'd wanted to ask Peter that question, but hadn't. There'd seemed little point. He knew she'd been invited to spend the holidays with them, so he'd made sure he wasn't able to make it this year.

He finished his champagne and set the empty glass on a passing waiter's tray. He should be concentrating on his job, part of which involved disaster relief. Kashmir had suffered another earthquake recently, and the Canadian

High Commissioner had offered India his services. Garrett was hoping to get into Jammu and Kashmir, and from there, Pakistan-controlled Kashmir, so he could follow the trail of those aircraft parts. Once he'd gathered the final pieces of information, if CSIS chose to do so, it would be able to share his intel through Interpol.

What CSIS really wanted were the names of any Canadian connections that had been in discussions with someone in the government in Kashmir.

Sushri Vaid, one of the few female Indian government officials present, approached him. Her department handled healthcare. In her early forties, and wearing a royal blue sari trimmed in gold embroidery over a matching, short-sleeved choli, she was a stunningly beautiful woman. They'd met on a number of occasions and Garrett liked her. More importantly, he trusted her. She was quiet, plain-spoken, and very committed to women's rights. She offered him her hand, a privilege he knew was also an honor. Women rarely shook hands with men, and when they did, it was only at their initiation.

"Good evening, Mrs. Vaid," he said. It was considered impolite to immediately launch into a business discussion, particularly at a social event. "How are your children? The last time we spoke, your oldest had begun lessons in Sanskrit."

Her lovely, kohl-lined eyes lit with pleasure as they exchanged stories about her family and his nieces and nephew. No one paid any attention to them as they spoke. Sushri was a woman and he was a low-level bureaucrat. Their lack of importance suited them both.

"I can make the introduction to the deputy secretary you'd asked me about whenever you'd like," she finally said to him, keeping her voice soft so that it wouldn't carry.

Garrett had been waiting all evening to meet him. This particular gentleman was well known to have dubious connections and empty pockets.

He followed Sushri through the crowd to a group of men standing somewhat apart from the rest of the room. She singled out one of the men, greeting him with *Namaste*, pressing her palms together and offering a polite nod of her head.

"Alok Badal." She lowered her eyes in deference. "I would like for you to meet Mr. Garrett Downing of the High Commission. Mr. Downing is a relief worker from Ottawa who'll be spending time in Jammu and Kashmir, organizing deliveries of supplies. I was just telling him that you see very few Canadians in Srinagar."

Garrett inclined his head in acknowledgment of the introduction. Deputy Secretary Badal was a stocky man with two chins and a poor attitude toward women. Technically, Sushri Vaid outranked him. That appeared to have escaped his notice.

"On the contrary, I personally have met two Canadians in the past year," he said to Garrett.

Sushri had given Garrett the perfect neutral topic to broach first. It allowed him to ask numerous questions about travel, and the many different types of people who might pass through the region in the run of a year. The conversation continued with Sushri dropping two or three careful observations—all of which Badal felt the need to dispute. Within ten minutes, Garrett had the names he needed and the places the Canadians had stayed while in the Kashmir Valley.

After five minutes more, and having learned everything necessary about the province's shortages and the supplies Canada could provide, Sushri quietly interrupted.

"Mr. Downing, I have a few other people anxious to make your acquaintance."

Garrett excused himself and allowed Sushri to lead him away. When they were safely out of earshot, and in a relatively private corner of the large room, he stopped to thank her for her help. "That was well done, Mrs. Vaid."

Her cheeks dimpled. "Remember this if RAW ever comes to the High Commission for assistance."

It took him a second to process that this lovely, kind woman had manipulated him. RAW was the acronym for India's Research and Analysis Wing, which specialized in foreign intelligence gathering and counter terrorism. They were also tasked with protecting India's nuclear program.

He shouldn't be so surprised. Sushri was exactly the type of person intelligence services looked for—smart, circumspect, well educated, and not at all what she seemed. He'd entrusted her with what had appeared on the surface to be nothing more than a small favor, and now she, too, had the information he'd been seeking.

He was reminded, suddenly and painfully, with the ripping open of a thinly-scabbed wound, of Isabelle. He missed her. He missed her quiet humor and gentle smiles. He missed never knowing what she was thinking. Even the way she manipulated him. His chest constricted. Especially that. He regretted all the things that had been implied between them but never said. Some things needed to be spelled out with perfect clarity, no matter if the understanding was already there. He'd never told her he loved her.

It was just as well. She'd have used it against him. He'd have done the same.

He dragged his attention back to Sushri Vaid. He harbored nothing but admiration for her. She'd no doubt gathered a great deal of intel from the deputy secretary that he'd missed, all because he'd underestimated her and hadn't picked up on what she was doing. He'd have to replay the conversation later to see if he could figure out what it might be.

"I'll remember this very well," he assured Sushri, but with an inflection of rueful humor to show there were no hard feelings. She had her job to do. He had his. Besides, she'd gotten him what he needed. He could hardly begrudge her if she'd gotten the same.

Sushri excused herself. Absently, Garrett followed the path of her striking blue-and-gold sari with his eyes as she worked her way through the throng of drab business suits. Here and there, a few other guests also wore colorful traditional dress, but for the most part, she stood out. And yet she was also invisible.

That was why she reminded him so much of Isabelle.

Suddenly, the gaudy decorations in the room made him tired and he was ready to call it a night, although his thoughts were guaranteed to keep him awake until the early hours of the morning. He exited the reception and stepped out onto Shanti Path, the street on which Canada's High Commission offices were located, and where his driver was waiting. He'd decided early on that the city's traffic was a bigger challenge than he was willing to embrace.

It was winter in New Delhi. The air cooled considerably once the sun went down, and he shrugged into the overcoat he carried. He'd opened the car door and was easing into the backseat, sinking into the plush leather cushions, when his cell phone rang inside his suit jacket. He fumbled for it, checking the number as he answered, and saw a Canadian area code.

It was his RCMP friend in Ottawa.

"Hey, Garrett," his friend said, with no hint of urgency,

and Garrett relaxed. Whatever was happening, it was nothing earth-shattering. "That passport you wanted me to keep an eye on. It showed up at the airport in Halifax, checking in for a midnight flight to Amsterdam."

Or maybe it was.

He stared out the dark-tinted window of the car, lost in thought. This late at night, traffic wasn't as great an ordeal. The drive to his flat took twenty minutes. By the time he got there, he'd made up his mind. He had to go to Jammu and Kashmir, yes. He had obligations to the High Commission and relief work couldn't wait. But many of the preliminary arrangements for supplies could be handled by phone. He'd delegate the rest.

First, he was going to Amsterdam.

CHAPTER THIRTEEN

ISABELLE CHECKED IN AT the small boutique hotel on Hooftstraat her father had booked for her, not far from the Rijksmuseum. It was where they usually stayed when he had the money to pay for it.

The concierge knew her by name. "He hasn't registered yet," he told her when she asked after her father. "He left a message for you saying he'll be out of the city for a few days, and that you're to wait for him."

"Thank you."

She crossed the foyer to the tiny lift and punched in her access code for the floor of her room. The hotel was very old and its architecture unique. Walls and ceilings slanted at whim. Furniture and doors appeared in unlikely locations. The overall effect was charming, and surprisingly functional.

She unlocked her door and saw at once that her father had arranged for a delivery to be left on her bed—clothes from PAUW, an exclusive Dutch fashion house, along with shoes and jewelry. *Because you deserve pretty things,* the accompanying note read. *Meet me for breakfast at the Rijksmuseum Café Tuesday at 09:30.*

The extravagance dismayed her, not because she

wasn't used to this from him, but that it came so close on the heels of months of hardship. She could think of far better uses for the money. She also recognized the gesture for what it was—an attempt to mollify her. How many times had she allowed him to do this very same thing, without question, in the past?

But Bangkok had scared her. So had Garrett, and the things her grandparents told her. None of it made her love her father any less. He was what he was. So was she, however, and she couldn't be part of his self-destruction anymore. She'd come here to tell him so.

Tomorrow was Tuesday. She'd meet him at the museum. Then she was going back to Canada to finish those four years of university if they killed her. Everything her father had purchased was being returned, and the money added to her tuition fund.

After a quick meal at a nearby café, she crawled into bed and slept for twelve hours straight.

When she awoke the following morning there was a light skiff of snow on the window ledge, but the sun was shining. She showered, then, ignoring the neat pile of new clothing, dug through the scant contents of her battered duffel bag. The nicest things she currently owned were her fleece-lined jacket and skinny jeans. Knee-high leather boots, not necessarily stylish but comfortable and warm, would also have to do. Rijksmuseum visitors came from all over the world and from all walks of life. No one in the café would notice—or care—what she wore.

She walked the short distance to the museum and entered through the bicycle tunnel beneath it. The glass and steel ceiling flooded the central Atrium with bright daylight that shone off the polished white stone floors. A short flight of stairs led to the open café overlooking the Atrium.

Isabelle looked up and spotted her father, sitting a few tables back from the guard railing. He lifted a hand and waved to her. A part of her had worried he might not be here, and the sight of him, alive and well, filled her with an overwhelming relief.

And then anger nipped at its heels. He'd chosen a very public place for an intensely private conversation. For months she'd been so afraid, both for him and herself, and yet here he was, acting as if he'd seen her yesterday, not almost a year ago.

As she mounted the stairs and wended her way through the tables, however, she began to see the changes in him. He'd always been an exceptionally handsome man, but while there was no mistaking the family resemblance, he drew attention whereas she did not. There was noticeable gray in his hair. His shoulders were more stooped than she remembered, and he'd put on weight. When he stood to welcome her, folding her into his arms to kiss her cheeks, she could read the deep lines etched around his eyes and the anxiety lurking in them. He scanned the floor of the Atrium below them as if looking for someone he hoped not to see.

"*Ma Belle*," he murmured, speaking in French. "I've missed you so much."

She slid into her chair and waited while her father ordered more coffee, and ham and cheese on bread. Once the waiter left, she immediately chastised him, also in French. "I was so worried. Where have you been?"

His hand, resting on the table, trembled slightly, and he couldn't quite meet her eyes. "It doesn't matter. I'm here now. You know I can't speak of my work."

Then, changing the subject, he launched into a long, very detailed description of all the things they would do together while they were in Amsterdam.

It took a moment for her to grasp the importance of what he wasn't saying. A frisson of anger chased away her disappointment in him. He planned to give her no explanation for his disappearance. Neither did he want to know what it was like for her to be stranded in Southeast Asia, then Canada, without any means of survival. He'd always been this way. He simply wasn't capable of dealing with confrontation, or the complex emotions accompanying it.

She managed to cut him off after the waiter delivered their fresh coffee and food. "I have work and school, Papa. I had to claim a family emergency to get this time off. I can only stay for a few days."

Her father's expression went blank for a second, then cleared. "You don't have to go back to Canada. I have money now."

"But how long will it last?" she asked gently. "I'm an adult. It's better for me to build a life of my own. I can't expect you to keep on providing for me."

She'd offended him.

"You're my daughter. I've always provided for you. I intend to keep on doing so. My work is more stable. The money is better. The past few years have been difficult, yes, but that's behind us."

"So what do I do the next time you disappear for months? How long am I supposed to wait for you, wondering if you're dead or alive?"

"Don't be ridiculous, Isabelle," he snapped. He set down his heavy porcelain coffee cup with such force that it rattled the saucer. "I've never let you starve in all your twenty-four years."

Blood began to pound in her ears, its roar dulling the noise from the milling crowd in the museum Atrium. He refused to acknowledge the truth—that her grandparents had seen to her care, and her mother's, for the first years of her life. That she'd taken on work as an au pair once she'd finished school because he was traveling so much and been short on funds. There had been plenty of cash flow problems in between as well. Many moves in the middle of the night. Those desperate weeks in Bangkok, and even with the Mansfords, were especially difficult for her to forget. If not for Garrett, her situation could easily have become very ugly.

She could see the escalating pattern of irresponsibility, not to mention the wear of the past few months on her father's health. Whatever he was involved in, it was growing more complicated, not less. It had cost her any hope for a relationship with Garrett. That particular pain squeezed at her heart, leaving her momentarily breathless, but she pried it loose and pushed it away. She'd gotten past it before. This wasn't the time to try and subdue it again. She had to move forward.

"I'm going back to Canada," she heard herself saying. "For twenty years my grandparents didn't know what happened to me. I'm not going to walk away from them again. They've already lost their daughter."

"And because of them, I lost my wife. Why should I allow them to take my daughter from me, too?" His expression hardened. "Don't feel sorry for them, Belle. They never wanted us in their lives. They made that clear."

They'd made no secret of the fact they had no love for her father, true enough, but he had none for them either, and Isabelle had no intentions of becoming caught in the middle of a decades-old feud. They didn't have to deal with each other in order to have a relationship with her. She wasn't a child, anymore.

A loud bang in the Atrium caused them, and everyone

seated around them, to jump, then turn and look. Isabelle heard the heavy tread of running footsteps, then loud apologies spoken in American English. It sounded as if something glass had shattered on the stone floor.

She shifted her gaze back to her father and saw he'd gone very pale. The trembling in his hands had worsened so that he'd spilled his coffee across the table. Isabelle grabbed their napkins and began to sop it up, her thoughts racing to an inevitable conclusion that she'd known, but in many ways was too much his daughter to admit.

He was afraid for his life. That was why he'd arranged for such a public place to meet her in, not because he hadn't wanted to deal with her disapproval. She'd looked the other way too many times over the years. She'd been too indulgent of his *laissez-faire* ways. She'd facilitated them. Now she had no idea how to help him. Arguing with him would solve nothing. Neither would any attempt to use reason. He was well beyond all that.

Garrett would know what to do.

The thought crept, unbidden, into her head. But he'd already tried to warn her, and when she hadn't listened, he'd washed his hands of her. She'd have to deal with this alone.

"Why don't we go back to the hotel, where it's quiet?" she suggested. "Have you registered yet?"

His hands had steadied, although his color concerned her. "I'm staying at a different hotel this visit." He offered no explanation as to why, or which one it was. Before she could ask, he changed the subject. "Since we're here, we may as well see the exhibits."

They spent the rest of the day wandering through the galleries. Late in the afternoon, he glanced at his watch and suggested they go out to dinner.

"You can meet me at the restaurant," he said. "First, go

change into one of those pretty dresses I bought you. Oh, I almost forgot." He reached into an inner pocket of his suit jacket and withdrew a small packet of papers. "I need this delivered. I'd do it myself, but I have a meeting I'm going to be late for. I was so happy to see you, I lost track of time. It's not far out of your way—just a few streets over from Hooftstraat."

The desperate, haunted look in his eyes betrayed him. As Isabelle accepted the packet, she wondered how many times he'd lied to her over the years. Even though she felt certain this was the first he'd tried to include her in his activities, ultimately, it didn't matter. She thought of the things Garrett claimed her father had done, of the lives already lost because of them, as well as the ones to come. She couldn't live with that on her conscience.

She couldn't imagine how her father lived with it, either. Or the fear. Espionage was a dirty game.

"I'll see you at seven," she managed to say, surprised by how light her voice sounded when inside, her heart was breaking.

She had to call Peter and Cheryl and ask them to help her contact Garrett. She was going to turn her father in.

Garrett waited in the cold outside the small, very exclusive, extremely discreet hotel. The winter days were short, and despite the early hour, dusk had already descended on the narrow streets. After the warmth of India, the damp chill in the air settled deep in his bones. He stuck his hands in the pockets of his overcoat and hunched his shoulders.

Isabelle wasn't inside. He'd asked the reticent

concierge to leave her a message for him, and if she'd been in her room, she would have responded to it immediately. He'd been explicit about the urgency.

He wondered if she'd be happy to see him. They'd parted on friendly enough terms.

No. Not friendly enough. And definitely not the terms he'd wanted. He'd made a mistake in walking away from her. He planned to rectify that. Either they became much more than friends or they'd be nothing at all. While he couldn't offer her reassurances over the fate of her father, he'd already distanced himself from that part of the investigation. He hoped that would suffice. It was the best he could do.

He straightened as he caught sight of her in the glow of the street lamps, crossing the bridge over the canal running behind him and then turning onto the street where he waited. His heart beat a little faster. He'd recognize her anywhere, simply by the way she moved. Her head was uncovered, and pinpoints of snow settled onto her dark hair, melting almost instantaneously.

He was nervous, but it was too late to worry. He stepped forward, blocking her path as she approached.

She looked up. Her expression blanked as if she couldn't quite process what she was seeing.

Then, with an exclamation in French of such intense relief he couldn't begin to interpret it, she threw herself into his arms. She hugged him, pressing her face against his throat. "Garrett! Thank God you're here."

Although he'd hoped she'd be happy to see him, this was a far more exuberant reception than he'd expected from her. He held her close, almost hating to ask why, but common sense and past experience had already weighed in with an opinion. Something was very wrong.

He looked around, unsure what to expect. A busy street

wasn't the best place to talk. They were drawing far too much attention. "Can we go inside?" he asked. "I've been out here for hours and I'm frozen."

She gripped his hand as they entered the hotel, edging her slender fingers between his so that they interlocked, as if she were afraid he'd vanish if she didn't hold onto him.

As soon as the door to her room closed behind them he pinned her against it, cupped her face in his hands, and kissed her. Her cheeks were so cold. So was the tip of her nose. He wanted nothing more than to peel every layer of clothing off her body and make love to her, slowly, for the rest of the night, warming them both.

She couldn't seem to stop touching him. Her hands dipped into the warmth of his coat, smoothing the front of his shirt as if reassuring herself he was real. He lifted his head and searched her eyes. He saw happiness in them, but also something else. Darker.

He shucked his coat and dropped it on a chair by the window, then settled his palms on her hips. The hot water radiator gurgled as the heat kicked in.

"I've missed you so much," he said. A trace of humor slipped into his tone. "Now. Why don't you tell me what's happened?"

She evaded his question. "Why are you here?" Her eyes narrowed. "How did you know where to find me?"

"I have my ways. And I've come for you."

"For me?"

The surprise and suspicion on her face hurt him. He should have told her how he felt about her long before this. But he remembered her words outside, on the street when she first saw him, and that was enough to warn him that now wasn't the right moment to tell her he loved her. *Thank God you're here* could mean a number of things, but it didn't speak to him of a desire for intimacy.

"If you're worried that I'm really here because of your father, the answer is, I'm not. My work's taken me in a different direction these days." He couldn't tell her everything, but he refused to give her false hope. "That doesn't mean he's been forgotten."

She unzipped her jacket and withdrew a packet of papers. She held it for a long moment, staring at it, then straightening her shoulders, she handed it to him. "Here. I was asked to deliver these for him. I'd planned to look at them first, but I'd rather you do it for me. I don't want to know what they contain."

Garrett took the packet. Inside, sandwiched between sheaves of paper, was a lump the size of a thumb drive. He hoped she understood what she was doing. "You realize," he said slowly, "that if these contain anything of interest to Canada, or Interpol, or the Netherlands, I'll have to report it?"

She nodded. "I'd planned to call you right after I'd looked at them. I didn't know what else to do." Her chin quivered. "He was so afraid when I saw him today, Garrett."

He unwound the string holding the packet folded in half and slid his finger under the flap of the envelope. He scanned the contents with a sinking heart. These were rough designs from a Canadian defense contractor that specialized in state-of-the-art surveillance equipment, catering to law enforcement agencies all over the world. He guessed the thumb drive would contain the design specifics. His next step would be to call his agency in Ottawa, who'd contact Interpol, who in turn would alert the Dutch National Constabulary, since the exchange was taking place in their jurisdiction.

"Where were you supposed to deliver these?" he asked.

Isabelle gave him the address. "Is it bad?"

"Bad enough." He rifled through the papers. These weren't plans for weapons of mass destruction, or weapons systems either, which came as a relief, but he couldn't say for certain what was on that thumb drive. And Isabelle said her father seemed afraid. That was bad, too. He tucked the papers back in the envelope and tied it shut. "At the very least, it's going to mean jail time for him. Are you prepared for that?"

"Of course not." She shivered, although she still wore her jacket and the room wasn't cold. "But I'd rather he be in jail and alive."

She said that now. She might feel differently in a few weeks or months. It was also very likely she might never be able to look at Garrett again without experiencing some level of remorse, remembering how he'd encouraged her to help put her father behind bars.

His hopes for a happy resolution to their relationship— or lack of one—evaporated.

"I have a few phone calls to make," he said.

He said he'd come for her.

He hadn't explained, or said anything more, and Isabelle hadn't dared ask what he meant. If she'd somehow misunderstood, she couldn't bear it. If she'd understood correctly, they were both destined for disappointment. Any connection to her would prove disastrous for his career. She'd never do that to him.

Right now, it was enough for her that he was here.

The restaurant where she was to meet her father had been converted from an old warehouse dating back to medieval times. The building was tall and narrow, deeper than it was wide. The topmost floor had once been living quarters. She believed the owner had turned it into a private penthouse. The three lower levels were dining rooms of varying degrees of exclusivity. She'd been here before, on numerous occasions. The chef was an acquaintance of her father's, and kept a personal table reserved for friends. She paused at the door of the topmost restaurant, sick to her stomach and hating what she was about to do.

She caught sight of her reflection in a mirrored wall, startled by it. On the outside, she looked so calm. She'd fastened her hair in a careless knot on the top of her head. A few tendrils wisped around her ears and the nape of her neck. Pearl drop earrings that had once belonged to her mother were a gift from her grandmother. She'd chosen a simple, thigh-length dove-gray tunic over black leggings, paired with high-heeled, black leather, over-the-knee boots, because they were all items she could wear again. Everything else her father had bought for her would go back to the store. She'd donate the money. She couldn't bear the thought of profiting from it.

Her unsettled stomach disagreed with the mirror's assessment of serenity. Garrett's presence outside on the street, and the two Dutch *politieagenten* she knew were somewhere inside, were all that kept her from bolting. She'd been given one opportunity to convince her father to turn himself in before the arrest. To keep this nightmare from happening. It was now or never.

The plan was simple. Partway through dinner, Garrett would enter so he could offer his support without interfering. She had no idea how he'd managed to arrange that. Tables were notoriously hard to reserve. She was to return the papers to her father and tell him she hadn't been able to deliver them. The *politie* wanted them on him when he was arrested. While CSIS dealt in information, law enforcement agencies preferred to have hard evidence that would stand up in court. After dinner, she was to find an excuse to leave the restaurant without him. Hopefully, he'd never learn of her involvement. The *politieagenten* would then make the arrest outside, when he was alone, as quietly as possible. If her father's life was truly in danger, they wanted no one to witness it, although Garrett had warned her it was unlikely to go without notice.

She walked through the open restaurant doors. This floor of the building had retained much of its original construction. Three walls were of brick, interlaid with tiles of *Delfts blauw*. Broad, roughhewn beams in the low ceiling had long ago grayed with age. Solid plank floors, worn in places, sagged in others.

The dining room had ten tables, elegantly dressed. Eight were occupied, most by couples. Two of the tables had four occupants, obvious business associates. Nowhere did she see two men alone. Perhaps the *politieagenten* hadn't yet arrived. Or they hadn't been able to secure a table.

Her father stood as she approached. The maître de held out her chair for her to be seated.

"You look beautiful," her father said to her, taking his seat again.

Garrett had already told her the same thing, but with a far different inflection. The memory of the light in his eyes as he'd offered his approval still warmed her.

They talked of inconsequential things. Her impressions of Bangkok. Nova Scotia. How much running they'd done over the past year, and if their times had improved. It was as if their lives hadn't changed at all. But they had. Their relationship wasn't what it had once been. Isabelle knew that, after this evening, it never would be again.

The main course was delivered. They ate it in silence. If her father was worried, she could no longer tell. Preoccupied, yes. But then, so was she. Garrett had arrived partway through the meal. She'd seen him out of the corner of her eye, being seated at an empty table near the front window overlooking the street, and lost what little appetite she'd had to begin with.

She refused dessert. Her father ordered another drink.

"Did you deliver the package?" he asked once their plates had been cleared.

She removed the papers from the black-sequined clutch resting on her lap and laid the packet on the table between them. "No. I was hoping you'd reconsider."

"Those papers aren't mine."

"They're in your possession."

Her father met her eyes. "They were in your purse. Anyone watching would have seen it."

The room spun. She gripped the edge of the table until it righted itself. This man was the stranger she'd been warned of, but had never met.

"Really, Papa?" she asked softly. "This is how you choose to deal with this?"

His eyes shuttered. "I have no other choice. It seems I've been abandoned by yet another Anjelais."

Inside, her heart was breaking. Garrett had tried his best to prepare her for this. He'd said she couldn't allow her father to make her feel guilty. That this wasn't a situation of her making. If she retreated now, and someday he ended up dead, then yes, she would be at fault.

"You have choices," she said.

"So do you. If you walk out of here without those papers, I'll know what yours is."

And now she knew his. Unshed tears burned the backs of Isabelle's eyes. She stood, fighting them off. "I love you, Papa."

He remained seated, unmoved by her emotion. "The people who love me don't leave me."

This, from the man who'd abandoned her in Thailand without a penny to her name. She didn't recognize him. Her heart cracked a little more.

She skirted the table, stooping, with a hand on his shoulder, to press a kiss to his cheek. "Good-bye."

She saw nothing as she departed the dining room, the empty clutch in her hand. She had no idea if Garrett followed her, or if the elusive *politieagenten* watched her exit. She wanted to get back to her room, gather her things, and return to Nova Scotia on the next flight.

She was so lucky that Garrett had found her grandparents for her. That he was with her, right now. At least she wasn't alone.

The same couldn't be said for her father.

CHAPTER FOURTEEN

ISABELLE WAS LEAVING THE restaurant.

Every male eye in the room had turned to watch her, some discreetly, a few with open appreciation. The outfit she'd chosen, while simplistic, screamed an attitude of elegant indifference. The tall, high-heeled boots, paired with the soft, thigh-grazing tunic, underscored the length of her legs and the athletic slenderness of her body. Subtle makeup brought out the curve of her cheeks and the exotic dark beauty of her eyes. She really was an extraordinary chameleon. Garrett would never forget how badly he'd underestimated her in Thailand, all because she'd chosen to go unnoticed.

Right now, the expression on her face gave nothing away. Not to anyone who didn't know her. Garrett, however, had learned that the less expressive she was, the more deeply she was troubled. He knew, without being told, that her father had hurt her.

He'd observed Beausejour throughout dinner. He was used to studying people, learning what motivated them. He'd seen no signs of the fear Isabelle had said her father had exhibited so plainly that morning. Instead, Garrett discovered where Isabelle got her talent for hiding her thoughts and emotions. Marc Leon Beausejour was an actor. A very good one, in fact. Garrett suspected Isabelle had been well played.

Beausejour was about to get what he so richly deserved. Isabelle, on the other hand, was not.

Garrett gave her a head start, then tossed some euros on the table and followed her. Once he was out of the dining area and out of sight, he collected his overcoat and ran down the steep flight of stairs, taking them two at a time, unmindful of the risk to his neck.

She was waiting for him on the street outside, staring at the brightly lit houseboats on the canal. Everywhere, the city sparkled with white, pinpoint lights that had been draped from trees, building canopies, and along the canals in preparation for the feast of *Sinterklaas* on December 6th.

He took Isabelle's hand, weaving their fingers together.

"This is it?" she asked, lifting her gaze from the water. She searched his eyes. "I don't have to do anything more?"

"Not a thing," Garrett assured her. "The police will handle it from here." He hated seeing the shell-shocked blankness on her face. It worried him. "Let's get away from here. I know of a wine bar nearby. We could both use a drink."

They walked in silence, one of many couples out for an evening stroll. The wine bar was full, but the seating arranged so as to be intimate and discreet. There were a few available stools at various bars scattered about, but Garrett slid the hostess twenty euros and asked for a place they could sit in private. They waited almost fifteen minutes, during which time Isabelle stared off into space and Garrett never let go of her hand.

They were eventually shown to two plush leather chairs drawn close together, the kind one could sink into, near a fireplace. A small round table nestled between them. Garrett ordered two *pinots noir*.

Isabelle took a sip of her wine. She was too calm. Too emotionless. His worry grew.

"I never saw the police," she said, startling out of her trance. "Are you certain they were there?"

"They were seated at the table nearest the door. You had to walk right past them on your way out. They would have been on your right."

"The blonde woman and the man in the pink shirt?" He nodded, and a small laugh escaped her. "No wonder I missed them. I was expecting two men."

"I seem to recall getting in trouble with you and Cheryl for being sexist," he teased her. "Just for that, you owe me a weightlifting session. Spot me and we'll call it even."

A glimmer of humor—and life—returned to her eyes. "You're rather trusting with your personal safety. Aren't you afraid I'll drop the weights on you?"

"Maybe you give me more credit than I deserve. I'm out of practice. I haven't done any real bench pressing in months."

"Thank you," she said suddenly.

"For what?"

"For insisting I make plans for my future. For finding my grandparents so I won't be alone. You knew this was coming, with or without my involvement."

"I'm glad you understand that his arrest was inevitable." Garrett twirled the glass in his hand, watching the dark red liquid dance in the firelight. "He knew the risks."

"At least he's safe." She set her untouched glass of

wine on the table between them. "Why do you suppose he got involved in such a business?"

It was impossible to understand men like Beausejour. That he believed himself cleverer than most people went without saying. Perhaps he was. What he failed to grasp was that him being clever didn't mean others were stupid. Garrett suspected that, when investigators began to peel away all the layers of his activities, they'd discover Beausejour was far more involved in foreign interference than anyone had realized.

"It's always about money. Never forget that. But most people in his line of work thrive on the excitement, as well. They're risk takers. The bigger the risk, the greater the payoff."

A puzzled frown formed between her eyebrows, tugging at the graceful arches. "Why would he have given me those papers?"

Truth be told, that bothered Garrett, too. He might have been testing her, to see if she'd follow instructions without question. More likely he'd intended to pull her deeper into his life and keep her close to him.

She turned dark, tragic eyes to his. "Do you suppose he wanted to be arrested?"

It was a possibility Garrett hadn't considered, and if it gave Isabelle comfort to believe it, then he saw no reason to suggest otherwise. "Anything's possible."

He leaned over to touch her cheek with the tip of his finger, unable, as always, to resist the smooth allure of her skin. He loved touching her and had no idea how long it might be before he got another opportunity. She'd be on the next flight to Nova Scotia. He was back to India.

He couldn't confess how he felt about her now, when she was vulnerable and he'd be so far away. He'd give her a few months. Surely, by then she'd know if she could stand the sight of him. But this time, he'd stay in contact with her. He wouldn't leave other people to watch over her for him.

Tonight, he didn't want her to be alone. He also didn't want her unprotected. Not until they knew the magnitude of her father's activities. He'd help her gather her things and he'd take her to his hotel for the night. His room had two beds, if that was what she preferred. Tomorrow, he'd drive her to the airport. A flight for Canada was scheduled to leave at midmorning.

The full force of the evening finally sank in. He could tell the moment her numbness wore off and the self-doubt hit her, and the exact instant recriminations began. Her eyes widened, her lashes fluttering a few times. She looked at him in stark panic. "Did I do the right thing?"

"Yes," Garrett said. "You did." He lifted her glass and handed it to her, pressing it into her fingers. "Finish your drink. Then, we're leaving."

Isabelle packed her bag under Garrett's watchful eye. She could feel his concern, and his calm, solid presence reassured her as nothing else would have.

She bundled the things her father had bought for her together and left a note for the concierge, who wasn't at his desk, asking him to please take everything to a consignment store and donate the money to a charity of his choice. She didn't wish to deal with returning them herself.

There was no need to check out. Her passcode would change automatically.

The hotel Garrett had registered in was part of an

international chain. Its rooms were the same the world over. It was spacious, comfortable, and impersonal. Its true appeal to her right now was that it contained Garrett.

She washed the makeup off her face and brushed her teeth in the bathroom, then donned her nightdress. She drew the pins from her hair, and with automatic motions, brushed it smooth. The aftereffects of adrenaline, and the glass of wine, left her mentally exhausted.

When she emerged from the bathroom, Garrett had already exchanged his suit and tie for a pair of cotton drawstring pajama bottoms. His broad chest was bare, and his hair mussed as if he'd used his fingers to comb it. He'd shut off the lights and now stood at the floor-to-ceiling window with the curtains thrown back so that the glittering city spread out before them.

She wanted to know why he was here. She wanted to hear him say the words out loud.

He turned when she entered the room, placing his back to the window and leaving his face in shadow. "You can take whichever bed you like."

She stopped at the foot of the one closest to him. "You said you'd come for me. Why?"

The room was silent other than for the muted voices from a television next door.

"This isn't the right time," he said finally.

She had to agree. But she didn't see how there was going to be a better one. The sooner they cleared the air between them, the easier it would be to go their separate ways. She loved him. Over and over, he'd proved himself to be everything her father was not. He had a family who adored him. He was deeply committed to the work he did and the integrity of the organization he worked for. Even though he'd been motivated to find out about her father, the truth was, he simply hadn't been able to leave a young woman stranded on the streets of Bangkok. She'd never have any reason to question him.

But loving her would be a mistake on his part. He was every bit the risk taker he said men like her father were. He simply chose to take his risks on the right side of the law, and on behalf of his country. He'd been attracted to her from the first because she'd posed a challenge to him. He couldn't figure her out.

Now he had. She'd lied to him too many times for him to ever truly trust her. He'd never be able to forget who—what—her father was. Neither would CSIS. And sooner or later, when he missed an assignment or promotion because of her, he'd come to resent her. She didn't want that to happen.

She moved closer to him and placed a palm on his chest. "How can you stand to look at me right now?"

He seized her hand in his so that she couldn't withdraw it. "What the hell are you talking about?"

Her heart was beating so fast it hurt to speak. "Will I always remind you of the things my father did? Of what he is?"

"Isabelle." His tone gentled. "When I look at you, I see nothing else at all, only you. Who or what your father is has no bearing on the way I feel about you. Not now, and not in the future. Don't ever think otherwise."

She wished she could believe that, but didn't dare. "You forget that when you first met me, I was trying to sell my passport."

"I met a woman who was fearless and resourceful, if somewhat misguided. Through no fault of your own, you'd been abandoned in a third-world country. So many things could have gone wrong and yet you survived. I don't want you to end up in that type of situation ever again. But again, this isn't the right time for us to be having this discussion. We both have too much going on in our lives."

She understood what he was trying to say, and knew he was right. He loved her, and she loved him, but they couldn't be certain it was going to be enough. "What happens next?"

"Tomorrow, you go back to Nova Scotia. I have an assignment to finish." He made a rueful face. With his thumb he began to massage the palm of her hand, an absent-minded but very erotic motion that melted every bone in her body. For the first time since dinner, she could actually feel. "You have no idea what I had to do to be here."

"I don't want you jeopardizing your work for me." But she was so grateful he had. She didn't know what she would have done without him. The cold man she'd had dinner with had shaken her. She'd always seen her father as weak. For the first time she'd glimpsed the person her grandparents claimed him to be.

"Nothing's been jeopardized," Garret said. "But I can't delay it any longer, either."

He released her hand and cupped her face in his palms, sliding his fingers into her hair, then kissed her with increasing hunger. Welcome sensation washed through her. She skimmed the pads of her thumbs over the hard plane of his stomach. She felt the hard length of his erection against the heel of one hand. She eased her fingers beneath the drawstring of his pajamas, stroking him with her palm.

He pressed his forehead to hers, his breathing ragged. "It's been a difficult day for you. This wasn't how I'd intended to end it."

Tomorrow was going to be even more difficult. She didn't want him to leave her.

"I'd prefer not to sleep alone tonight," she said, "but I'm not going to force myself on you."

A low chuckle rumbled deep in his chest. "How honorable of you. Unfortunately, I don't have your impressive level of self-control. I've spent too many lonely nights thinking about you."

He nudged her backward until her knees collided with the edge of the bed and she toppled onto the mattress. He landed on top of her, his hands on either side of her head to carry his weight, and kissed her again until she was breathless.

Afterward, she nestled against him, his arm thrown across her and holding her tight to his chest. She'd thought she wouldn't be able to sleep. Instead, she drifted off almost at once.

The next morning, Garrett navigated his rental car through the heavy traffic in Haarlem as if he'd lived in the city his whole life. He'd done far more international travel than he let on, that much was obvious.

She stared out of the passenger window as they passed through a tunnel under one of the many canals. They'd already talked about what would happen next for her father. The Canadian government would begin an extradition process. The Dutch government might or might not appeal it, since the crime he'd be charged with initially had taken place on their soil. Either way, Garrett had given her a phone number so she could inquire about her father's welfare, but he'd cautioned her not to use it too frequently. He'd called in a favor to get it for her.

"He's a flight risk," Garrett had also warned her. "He'll be held under anti-terrorism laws and not granted bail."

When they reached Schiphol airport, he followed the signs to the entrance for the underground parking lot. Minutes later, he was taking her bag from the trunk and they were winding through the maze of parked cars toward the elevators. He waited as she checked in at one of the many self-serve kiosks scattered throughout the main terminal.

After she'd dropped off her bag with the airline, and before she headed into the international departures area, he folded her in his arms and held her. She curled her fingers into the lapels of his coat, breathing in the familiar smell of his aftershave.

"This isn't good-bye," he murmured into her hair. "I'll see you in a few months. I'll call you whenever I can."

She didn't want him to know how scared she was at the prospect of being so long without him. She had to be more self-sufficient and try to build a life of her own. The thought depressed her. "Will somebody be waiting for me when I land in Canada to take my passport from me this time, too?"

"There's no need for that." He grinned down at her, his hazel eyes warm. "I've got you flagged in the system. You can't make a move without me knowing about it."

"Flatterer." She should be upset with him, but she wasn't. It felt too good to know that he cared. A whisper of sadness sighed through her. She didn't want what was between them to change. She didn't want him to always feel the need to keep track of her movements.

She didn't want him to grow to resent her.

Someone bumped into them, jostling them aside, then moved on without a word of apology. They were blocking traffic.

She untangled herself from his arms. "I should be going."

She'd only gotten a few feet, however, before she heard him calling her name. "Isabelle."

She paused and half turned, adjusting the strap of her shoulder bag so it wouldn't slip off her arm. He was watching her, a curious, conflicted expression on his face that made her suddenly nervous. "Yes?"

People were passing between and around them, indifferent to the electric charge in the air.

"I love you," he said, ignoring everyone else. "That's why I came for you. I thought maybe you should know, after all."

She had. It was nice to hear.

He strode away before she could find the right words to respond.

CHAPTER FIFTEEN

Halifax, Nova Scotia, May

IT HADN'T BEEN THE most romantic declaration of love ever made. He hoped to do better this time. Her reaction, or lack of it, had left him concerned.

It was a Saturday night. The low-ceilinged tavern where Isabelle worked was crowded and noisy. The band at the front was partway through their second set. Garrett paid the cover charge at the door, then found a place to stand near the bar where he could watch her as she waited on tables.

At first glance, and if one didn't look closely, they would see a woman of average appearance. Straight brown hair worn in a no-nonsense ponytail. Brown eyes. Warm, pale-olive skin. It was the second, more careful look that held a man's attention. She had a way of moving—a tilt of her head, a subtle sway to her hips as she passed between the long tables—that was captivating. When people spoke to her, she listened to them with serious, undivided attention.

He liked the short kilt she wore, although he was fairly certain no Scottish clansman had ever sported anything even remotely similar.

So far, she hadn't seen him.

His work had taken longer than he'd expected. He'd called her many times over the past five months, but they'd never discussed the last thing he'd said to her before leaving her at the airport. Their conversations had been brief and centered on the little things happening in their lives. She told him about her classes and work. She'd spent Christmas with her grandparents in Quebec. He'd kept his talk about India vague, mentioning little things about his relief work in Jammu and Kashmir but nothing specific. He knew more about her father's case than she did, although he hadn't told her anything about it. She understood that he couldn't discuss it with her and so she didn't ask questions.

Marc Beausejour's arrest had turned out to be somewhat of a coup. He possessed several different identities and had traveled to Canada on numerous occasions over the years. It was shocking how easily altered passport photos could fool sophisticated facial recognition software, and the way the human eye will automatically see the person holding the document as matching the image. Security personnel examined hundreds of terrible passport photos in the run of a day. Garrett should have figured out something wasn't right when Isabelle had mentioned leaving with her father soon after her mother's funeral. It wasn't that simple for a single parent to take a small child out of the country. At least, it shouldn't have been.

It was going to take months of working with Interpol and other agencies for CSIS to unravel the extent of Beausejour's involvement in espionage and organized crime. The one thing Garrett had learned was that Beausejour had indeed sold stolen weapons systems to a dealer in Thailand, who'd then sold them to another dealer in India, and so on. The chain started in Canada and was long and complex, but in all the instances Garrett had explored, it led back to Isabelle's father. The Minister of Defence had turned out to be an old classmate and remained under a quiet, unofficial CSIS watch.

Garrett ordered a beer, the cold glass sweaty in the stifling room. It was the first of May in Nova Scotia, warm enough through the day for the outside deck to be open to customers, but still too cool at night to attract many patrons. It had been almost a year to the day since he'd first met Isabelle.

He'd missed her birthday. He knew Cheryl had taken her out for lunch because he'd asked her to. He had a gift for her in his pocket.

Isabelle started for the bar with an empty tray tucked under her arm and saw him. She stopped. Her eyes met his over the crowd. He read confusion, followed by a smile of such pure pleasure it set his heart on fire. He'd worried for nothing over how she'd react after all this time.

Within seconds, she was at his side. It was typical of her, however, that she did nothing to draw too much attention to them. She placed a hand on his arm, her fingers tightening, but that was it. He received no welcoming kiss. No outward show of excitement that anyone but him would discern. The look in her eyes was enough, however, at least for the moment.

"What are you doing here?" she asked.

"You always ask me that question. My answer's always going to be the same." He bent his head and whispered in her ear. "I came for you."

She swayed toward him, then checked herself. "You could have picked a better time and place."

He'd spent five days in Ottawa being debriefed. The minute he'd been dismissed, he'd taken the first available plane to Halifax. He wasn't waiting any longer to see her. "My flight just got in. I dropped my bags at the hotel and came straight here. I have a month to make up for bad timing." He didn't really. He had case files to study for his next assignment, but he could do that here as easily as anywhere. "When are you off?"

"Not for another hour."

"I'll wait."

The minutes dragged. Finally, Isabelle headed through a set of swinging doors bearing a sign that read STAFF ONLY. She returned moments later, wearing a tight zippered sweater over the brief Nova Scotia tartan. With those knee socks and ponytail, she looked like a schoolgirl. She was now twenty-five. He'd turned thirty-two three months ago. He couldn't decide if she were the embodiment of some secret fantasy, or if she made him feel old.

Both, he decided.

As soon as they were outside in the empty, poorly lit courtyard that led to the tavern, she threw her arms around his neck and kissed him. He stumbled against the side of the stone-faced building and held her tight, returning her kisses with a matching hunger. She slid a knee between his thighs, pressing closer.

"How far away is your hotel?" she demanded.

Too far, which was probably for the best. For the moment.

Garrett grasped her elbows and set her away from him so he could think again. He took hold of her hand. "Not just yet. First, we need to talk." He'd planned to sit on one of the many secluded benches along the boardwalk on the harbor front, but it was well past midnight, with a raw wind blowing off the water, and she wasn't dressed for it. "Let's go get something to eat."

They walked a few blocks to a restaurant. Inside, except for the bored staff, it was deserted. They were shown to a small booth at the back with a half-burned candle in a jar on the table.

Now that they were alone, he scarcely knew where to begin. Five months was a long time apart. Perhaps they should have gone to his hotel after all, and done their talking later.

"How were your exams?" he asked.

She made a face. "Boring."

He had to fight to keep from smiling. Isabelle wasn't an exceptional student. She did well enough, but only because she was bright. She had no enthusiasm for it. He was glad. It made the offer he was going to extend to her easier to make.

"You enjoy working with people. It so happens that my next position involves humanitarian relief. How would you like to go to Sierra Leone with me?"

Interest sparked in her eyes, followed by caution. "Would you be allowed to take me?"

"Why wouldn't I be? You haven't done anything wrong."

"I haven't, no." She looked at her fingers, lacing and unlacing them on a pristine white tablecloth washed in the glow of candlelight. "But we both know my father is going to be convicted."

He didn't deny it. She had no true idea yet of the extent of his crimes. "Why don't you tell me what you think it will mean for you if he is?" He probed a little deeper. "For us?"

"You have security clearances to think of. I can't possibly be good for your career."

"I disagree. I think you'd be excellent for it." He picked up her hand and held it in both of his. "You speak a number of different languages. You've traveled extensively and you enjoy it. You're good in a crisis. I think you'd enjoy relief work. I also think you'd do well in fundraising. Those are all skills I could find a use for."

A waiter came to the table. Garrett ordered two glasses of sauvignon blanc, which arrived a few minutes later.

"You want me to work for you?" Isabelle asked once they were alone again. She sounded disappointed.

"I want you to work *with* me," he corrected her. "But the pay will be terrible. It's more in a volunteer capacity." He reached in his pocket and withdrew a small, oblong box. "I missed your birthday. I have a gift for you."

She opened it, tugging off the ribbon and lifting the lid. Inside was a silver whistle. She held it up, a question in her eyes.

"It's a dog whistle," he explained. "I thought that might be more effective against coyotes than a lifeguard whistle the next time we go running at the farm. I've been training," he added. "I wanted to do something with you that I knew you'd enjoy."

"I…don't know what to say."

His heart hammered inside his chest. He needed to know what she was thinking. "Do you want to be with me, Isabelle?" he asked. "Do you want to travel with me, and go running with me, and plan a life together with me? Or have I been reading you all wrong?"

Her fingers clenched tightly around the whistle. A hint of tears sparkled in her eyes. She was so beautiful.

"You haven't been reading me wrong. I want those things more than anything. I wasn't sure if you wanted to have them with *me*."

He traced a finger along the curve of her cheek, swallowing hard. "I told you I'll always come for you. But I'd far rather take you with me."

"Cheryl and Peter have paid a lot of money toward my education. I can't just walk away from that." She must have seen the guilt on his face. Understanding dawned on hers. "*You* paid for it."

"And it was money well spent. At least now you know for certain what you don't want to do with your life." He withdrew a second box from his pocket. "I have another gift. This one isn't for your birthday. It's for mine. I chose my own. I hope you don't mind."

She opened the box. Inside was a square-cut, pink diamond solitaire that flashed in the candlelight. "It will look beautiful on you."

He laughed. "The ring's not my gift. I was hoping you would be." He took the ring from the box and held it between his fingers. "I love you. You don't have to say yes right away. You can take some time to think about it. But I'm hoping the next time I leave, you'll be with me. As my—"

"Yes," Isabelle interrupted, cutting him off. "I haven't needed to think about it since the night I called your bluff. I wanted you more than anything then, and I want you now. *Je t'aime*. I love you too, and I'm afraid if I wait to say yes, you'll change your mind." She set the box on the table and stared at it, biting her lip. "Are you certain this is what you want?"

"I've never been more certain of anything in my life. I'm not changing my mind." He reached for her hand and slid the ring into place. "I know things aren't going to be easy, especially in the next few months. I'm not directly involved in your father's investigation anymore, but if I uncover something that connects back to him, I'll have to report it. You understand that, don't you?"

"Will you be able to go with me once I'm allowed to visit him?"

"Absolutely."

She curled her fingers around one of his. "Then let's get out of here. We have a wedding to plan." She smiled into his eyes. This time, he had no difficulty reading what was in hers. "And a wedding night to practice for."

Garrett left money on the table for the two untouched glasses of wine. Out on the dark, narrow street, a loud group of drunken college students stumbled toward them. He put a protective arm around Isabelle, buffering her against them as they swarmed past.

Isabelle slid both her arms around his waist. She looked up at him, her face serious in the light from the restaurant's sign. "Do you remember how we first met in Khao San?"

"It's hard to forget. It's not every day you catch a girl selling a passport like a pro behind a shrimp cart." He didn't like remembering it, either. So many things could have gone wrong for her.

"I was so scared," she confessed. "I had no one to turn to. And then there you were, and I haven't been scared since. At least not for myself. Thanks to you, I have my grandparents back in my life. Cheryl and Peter treat me like one of the family. You can't imagine how much that means to me." She reached up to kiss him. "I know you've tried hard not to come between me and my father, and you haven't. He did that all on his own. If he chooses to be a part of my life again, and I hope someday he will, he'll have to do it on my terms, not his. And my terms include you. I won't keep secrets from you. I won't do anything that might hurt your career. If he wants to speak to me, he'll have to pick up the phone and call me. If he wants to see me, it will be with your knowledge."

She had nothing to prove to him. He didn't need reassurances from her. "I don't want to be your jailor,

Isabelle. You aren't my prisoner. I want to be your husband. That means trusting you, and I do."

"But after everything, and all that you know about me, how can you possibly?" she asked.

"How can I not? The nature of my work means I can't always be honest with you. I can't tell you everything. So you're going to have to trust me, too. I'm not going to ask that of you if I'm not willing to offer you the same thing. Besides," he held her a little tighter, wrapping his jacket around her for added warmth, "there's no reason not to trust you. You're very loyal. For instance, the bartender at your work. The blond guy who couldn't take his eyes off you all evening. He's asked you out, hasn't he?"

"I never accepted." She smiled up at him. "He isn't you."

He refused to feel jealous. "I rest my case."

"But I admit I was tempted," she added. "That was before Amsterdam, though."

He tamped down a second, hotter flare of jealousy. "Let's not get too crazy with the honesty. All I need to know is that you love me."

Her eyes softened. "I do. More than you can imagine."

"My imagination is good."

She took his hand, her face glowing with a smile so warm and genuine it made him forget his own name.

"Then let me show you."

At Isabelle's insistence, the wedding was small. They were married in Lac Saint-Pierre so her grandparents could attend. Garrett's parents were the only other guests.

As a compromise to the rest of his family, they spent

their first Christmas together at the Mansfords' farm in Nova Scotia. Garrett's parents joined them. So did Isabelle's grandparents. Isabelle and Garrett had agreed that they'd spend as many holidays as they could with their families. Her grandparents were elderly and wouldn't have too many more years to travel. Nova Scotia was as far as they'd venture.

Not so for Isabelle. Sierra Leone had been a challenge so far, and she loved every minute of it. She'd picked up a little Krio, the local lingua franca. She was looking forward to Brazil, too. Garrett was scheduled to spend the next year there and she planned to learn Portuguese.

Right now it was Christmas morning, and they had all gathered in the formal living room. Gifts had been opened. Colored scraps of paper were strewn around the enormous tree. Kiefer had attached himself to Isabelle's memère, much to her pleasure. Isabelle smiled at the picture they made. The little boy had his thumb in his mouth as her grandmother cradled him on her lap. He was still in his bright red pajamas. Memère, very French, had carefully dressed in a pale suit with a pastel blue scarf around her neck. Chelsea and Beth sat with Garrett's mother, Elizabeth Downing, and were excitedly explaining to her how to use their new karaoke machine.

Isabelle set the tray of coffee and cocoa she carried on the round oak coffee table in the center of the room. Garrett placed dessert plates and a basket of muffins and cutlery beside it. Cheryl and Peter were in the kitchen, making bacon and eggs. Later on in the day, everyone was headed to the main farmhouse for Christmas dinner with Peter's family.

"Overwhelmed?" Garrett whispered in her ear.

"A little."

She wouldn't trade this for anything. Yet, as happy as

she was with her new family, it bothered her that her father would never be welcome at these gatherings. She hated to think of him all alone. He'd loved the holidays.

"Want to try out your new snowshoes?" Garrett asked. They'd opted not to buy anything unnecessary or overly expensive for each other. He'd suggested snowshoes, which they could leave at the farm for their winter visits, because running on roads that could sometimes be icy wasn't always an option.

"I'd love to."

They trudged through the snow-covered fields until they came to a small path in the woods. Garrett rubbed the tip of his red nose with the back of his glove. "I have one more gift for you."

She frowned up at him as she tried to wiggle the tip of one snowshoe free of a tangle of underbrush. "We agreed not to do this."

"It's nothing big or expensive." He hesitated. "It's two plane tickets for tomorrow. I thought we'd fly to Ottawa for the day and visit your father."

The thoughtfulness of the gesture, combined with the wind whipping the snow in little whirlpools of white that stung her cheeks, had her blinking her eyes. Her father had been extradited to Canada the previous summer. His trial was scheduled for this coming March. Although she'd spoken to him a few times on the phone, she hadn't seen him since Amsterdam. She'd deliberately stayed away.

"Are you sure you don't mind?" she asked.

"Of course I don't. He's your father. Since I'm not likely to get his vote for son-in-law of the year any time soon, though, if he doesn't want to meet me, I'm good with that."

"I love you," Isabelle said. "You have my vote."

Garrett laughed. The sound of it never failed to send a hot jolt of pure pleasure through her. He was a completely different person when he was alone with her.

"Yours is the vote that matters the most. I love you, too." He tugged the hood of her parka more securely around her wind-bitten cheeks, then bent forward at an awkward angle over their toe-to-toe snowshoes to give her a kiss. "You're thinking something. What is it?"

She grabbed for the sleeve of his coat with clumsy, mittened fingers to keep from tipping over into the snow. "That if I'd known how much a Canadian passport was going to be worth to me in Bangkok, I'd never have waited two weeks to try and sell it."

Garrett's hazel eyes smiled into hers. "Just imagine how much it will be worth in another forty or fifty years. Its value is only going to appreciate."

Happiness soared through her. She'd be spending those years with Garrett. The future was no longer something to fear, but to look forward to.

"*Mais oui, mon cher*. I'm counting on it," she said.

THE END

NOTE TO READERS

Thank you for choosing *Her Spy to Have,* the first book in my *Spy Games* series. I hope you enjoyed reading Garrett and Isabelle's story as much as I enjoyed writing it.

Canada prides itself on its freedom of information policies and public disclosure, and CSIS, Canada's spy agency, isn't exempt. If you read the actual *Canadian Security Intelligence Act*, however, as Isabelle did, you'll note there's a great deal of ambiguity to their mandate, and my characters have chosen to exploit it. They are spies, after all.

Next up is Kale and Irina's story in *Her Spy to Hold*. These two have a far different relationship from Garrett and Isabelle. Even I was taken by surprise.

And the *Spy Games* series doesn't end here. The third book, *His Spy at Night*, is currently in the works.

OTHER CONTEMPORARY ROMANCE
TITLES BY
PAULA ALTENBURG

Spy Games series:
Her Spy to Have – Book One, available now
Her Spy to Hold – Book Two, coming in May 2016
His Spy at Night – Book Three, TBA

Broken Hearts series:
I'll Love You Forever – Book One, available now
Book Two – TBA
Book Three – TBA

From Tule Publishing:
Her Secret Love

From Entangled Publishing:
Her Secret, His Surprise
Desire by Design

Read on for an excerpt from *Her Spy to Hold*, Kale and Irina's story.

Excerpt from

HER SPY TO HOLD
KALE AND IRINA'S STORY

by Paula Altenburg

IRINA WAS COOKING DINNER when the knock came on her kitchen door.

She froze with the steel butcher knife she'd been using to chop green onions for an omelet suspended in midair. She wasn't expecting visitors.

She laid the knife on the wooden cutting block, then crossed the kitchen to the two-panel steel side door of her bungalow, the one that led to her carport, and peered through the curtain. All of her doors and windows were locked. The air conditioning took care of the summer heat and humidity.

Thor stood on her doorstep, hulking and blond, and scary.

He wore his hair in a man bun. The wide smile on his lips and the ridiculous courier uniform did nothing to offset the alarming effect of the shiny black eye and the darkening bruise on his forehead.

Adrenaline kicked her heartrate into high gear. She left the chain in place on the inner door, opening it only far enough so she could speak through the crack. The locked screen door added another layer of protection. It wouldn't stop him if he tried to force his way in, but it would slow him down enough for her to slam the inner door shut and shoot the deadbolt.

"You must have the wrong address. I'm not expecting a delivery."

"Dr. Irina Glasov? My name is Kale Martin. Detective Buchanan suggested I pay you a visit. He said you'd asked for a meeting." He fumbled in his shirt pocket for a piece of ID. He flipped it open and held it up.

She couldn't get a close enough look at it through the screen, not that it mattered. She'd never be able to confirm the legitimacy of it even if she did. Hope warred with suspicion. "Do you mind waiting a few minutes while I give Detective Buchanan a call to confirm it with him?"

The giant didn't take offense to her caution. "Not at all."

She left him on the doorstep while she dug her cell phone and the business card Detective Buchanan had given her out of her purse. She punched in the number.

As it turned out, the detective had, indeed, asked Mr. Martin to stop by. The description he gave her matched the man at the door, right down to the black eye, courier uniform, and running shoes, but Irina continued to hesitate even after she disconnected the call. While this seemed a little elaborate for a hoax, whoever had managed to hack into her computer wasn't trying to be subtle. The implicit threat had been frightening.

She wished she were taller and more assertive. A self-defense course wouldn't have been remiss, either. She'd let Mr. Martin in, but she'd stand at the counter so she'd have the butcher knife close at hand. She'd never be able to use it on anyone, but he didn't need to know that.

She slid back the chain and unlocked the screen door.

She didn't open it but retreated to the counter, leaving him to let himself in.

The Norse god stepped over the threshold, his sheer size swallowing what she'd considered a spacious kitchen. If he lifted his hand above his head he could plant his palm on the ceiling. Fine gold hairs sprinkled tanned calves and forearms. Bulging biceps and broad pectoral muscles strained the seams of the gray cotton, short-sleeved shirt. Faint blond scruff, caught in the light from the bay window, stubbled his jaw.

The guy was beautiful. She had a difficult time believing he was an intelligence officer. Weren't they supposed to blend in?

The only place he'd go unnoticed was Asgard.

ABOUT THE AUTHOR

Paula Altenburg lives in rural Nova Scotia, Canada, with her husband and two sons. Once a manager in the aerospace industry, she now enjoys working from home and writing fulltime. Visit her at www.paulaaltenburg.com to view more of her work and to sign up for her newsletter. You can also follow her on Twitter @PaulaAltenburg and friend her on Facebook: https://www.facebook.com/PaulaAltenburgAuthor/.